# TRAIN DEPOT ORPHANS

*The American West Series*

LAURA STAPLETON

Cover by Cheeky Covers

Edits by Aquila Editing

 Created with Vellum

## Acknowledgments

There really is a town named Madison, Missouri. Unlike my Madison town, the real place is terribly small, with a population between five and six hundred.

Also, did you know rural mail delivery began on October 1, 1896, in West Virginia? Soon in the story, Eldon will need to hire a mail carrier or two. If you want to read that book, too, let me know, and I'll be glad to write it.

## *Dedication*

*For Dirk. Thank you for tolerating my asking Google my research questions aloud while you're trying to work from home. Turns out, being stuck on a deserted island with you wouldn't be so bad after all.*

# CHAPTER 1

Dorothy McLean's hands shook as she put on her white gloves. Every day, except Sunday, meant mail day, which meant seeing Eldon Lukeson at the post office. He'd worked there since they were youngsters. She loved having the excuse to visit him so often to ask for the McLeans' mail. "Mother, I won't be long. Do I need to stop by the dry goods for you?"

Mrs. Junie McLean came into the parlor from the kitchen. "No, darling. Mattie Lou went this morning." She walked up to her daughter. "She could begin going to the post office for you, too."

The gentle smile of her mother's teased, and Dorothy's cheeks burned. "I need to go myself because one day, I'll arrive there to learn he has a wife, and I'll never need to struggle to greet him again." She picked up her tote bag.

"Once there's a Mrs. Eldon Lukeson to stop my silly madness, all of my shyness will fade."

Her mother tsk-tsked, asking, "Do you really believe that?"

Dorothy couldn't meet her mother's searching green eyes. Instead, she stared into the tote's empty space. "I want to, but no. I don't. I've adored him since we were in school together. One would think I'd have gotten over my girlish crush by now and said more than two words at a time to him, but no. He's just everything a man should be. Handsome, kind, strong. I've tried to find fault with him but can't." Realizing she was going on a little too much about her feelings for Eldon, she smiled and glanced at Junie. "So, I merely wait until he finds a much more conversational woman to sweep him off his feet."

Mrs. McLean put her arms around Dorothy. "My darling Dotty. One day you'll realize a man is just a man. As easily spoken with as me or anyone else you know well."

She leaned into her mother's hug. "Even Mr. Lukeson?"

"Especially Mr. Lukeson. Even he, the paragon of manliness that he is, still puts his pants on one leg at a time." She let go of her daughter. "Now then, bring me back a Godey's Lady's book because I have no idea of what to wear without them telling me the fall fashions."

Dorothy chuckled. The very thought of her mother not

having a clear vision of her wardrobe in any situation wasn't possible. Mrs. Dodger McLean, Junie to her friends, had all the brashness and bravery Dorothy so wished she'd inherited. "Very well. I'll be sure to demand your copy the instant I walk in."

Junie laughed, shaking her head. "Silly girl. I'd be happy with you politely requesting if it means talking to your handsome beau."

"Mother, please." Her face warmed as she went for the door. "He's a familiar person is all." Before Junie could argue, Dorothy hurried outside. The bright afternoon sun reminded her of her missing sunbonnet. She glanced back at the McLean home. A short walk to the post office couldn't hurt her skin too much.

Hurrying to the station, Dorothy kept her chin down a little. She'd grown up in Madison, Missouri, and knew everyone in town. Still, she didn't want to chat with folk too much. They'd expect her to participate in the give and take conversation required, except of course Mr. Allen. The crusty old gentleman at the livery was wonderful about doing all the talking for her.

Mr. Allen's lectures on the others in Madison taught her everything about Eldon since they'd stopped attending school together. How he was single, moved here from St. Louis, hunted or fished on the weekends. He always shared his catch with Mr. and Mrs. Allen. Dorothy nodded at Lily

Rogers, another former schoolmate of hers. The other young lady smiled, acting as if she were coming over before Dorothy ducked into the train station's post office.

Crisis averted, the crowded room both horrified and broke her heart. Seven children stood around Eldon. Every one of them cried as the youngsters clung to the older ones. The door closed behind her with a bang, capturing everyone's attention. When Eldon's clear blue eyes met Dorothy's, her brain stopped. His dark, almost black hair was ruffled, his shirt partially pulled from his waistband by a tugging child. Or so she assumed. The navy fabric had smudges as if one of the small fry had needed a handkerchief.

"Hello, Miss McLean," Eldon said just before the wailing resumed. A little louder than the group around him, he added, "May I help you?"

"I..." Dorothy began. His full-on gaze pinned her as her heart clawed its way to her throat. She coughed before saying, "I, um, see you need my help instead."

He grinned. "If you could summon your schoolteacher magic, I'd be forever grateful."

He knew about her work? Dorothy's mouth went dry. Of course he did. He hadn't needed to ask around town to figure out who was the only schoolteacher. "I, um, yes. I certainly can." She cleared her throat and used her classroom voice. "Children, there's nothing to be gained by crying. Please have a seat on the bench while Mr. Lukeson fetches us napkins for your noses."

Every child did as requested, and she took stock of each as they found a seat. Three girls and four boys sat in a row. Siblings were easy to spot since their coloring was similar. A couple of the youngest boys who appeared nothing alike leaned against each other. "Good afternoon. I am Miss McLean. Let's start at this end." She went to the oldest girl. "I'd like to know your name and your favorite animal."

As Dorothy had hoped, the question disarmed the girl a little bit. She glanced at her brother before answering. "I'm Mary, and I like birds the most."

"Hello, Mary. It's a pleasure to meet you," Dorothy responded to the olive-complected girl. She faced the boy next to her, who shared Mary's deep green eyes and black hair. "And you?"

"I'm Ralph, her"—he crooked his neck to Mary—"brother. I like lions and tigers."

"Excellent choices, Ralph." She stepped sideways to face the next child.

Before she could ask, Eldon came up with a handful of napkins. "I found these. They're clean and enough for each child to have one."

"Perfect, thank you," she replied, pushing away her shyness to focus on the children. Eldon began giving each youngster something to wipe their eyes and blow their nose with. When he knelt to help the smallest boy, her heart melted. Eldon would make such a good father someday. Even in school, he was always helping children in the lower grades with homework. He had taken the time to teach the younger boys without fathers how to fish and play catch.

Distracting Dorothy from her mooning over Eldon, the fair little doll of a girl next to Ralph offered, "Miss McLean? I'm just Lucia for now, and I'm not sure I have a favorite animal. I like birds, cats, dogs, but not rats."

The others voiced their agreement, and Dorothy nodded. Grateful for the girl's initiative, she said, "I feel the same. While I'm certain they have a purpose in our world, they're not my first pick." Another step brought her closer to Eldon and face to face with a boy as old as Mary if she had to guess. "What is your name, and do you have a favorite animal?"

"I'm William and chickens, I guess." He shrugged. "They taste good, I can train them, and I like eggs."

Eldon chuckled before hiding his laugh with a cough, and Dorothy smiled. "Good choice, William. Do you ever go by a nickname?"

He crossed his arms. "People try to call me Will or Bill, but I don't like it."

Dorothy nodded and glanced at Eldon. "I appreciate your telling me." Stepping to be in front of the next child, a girl who had the same hued skin of dusky taupe as William, she asked. "Are you his sister?"

The girl twisted a curl around her finger. "I am. My name is Juliet, and I don't like chickens."

"Oh?" Dorothy said, wanting to hear why Juliet would disagree with her brother's choice.

"They peck her every time," William offered before adding, "I didn't train them to, either."

Dorothy looked down at her feet to keep from laughing. "I'm proud of you, then. Juliet. I'm very glad to meet you."

Before she could go to them, one of the youngest boys stood, dragging his brother up off the bench with him. "I'm Robby, and this is Chas. We're twins. I'm hungry. So is he, but I'm the only one who needs to go to the bathroom. He's pretty quiet, so I do the talking for him." Robby looked at his brother, asking, "You don't mind, do ya?"

Chas shook his head. "I don't mind. He has more to say. I like horses best."

Robby stuffed the napkin in his pocket. "So do I. I want to ride horses someday. Take care of baby horses on me and Chas's farm."

"I'll show you where the restroom is," Eldon said, holding out his hand for Robby to take. "How old are you and your brother?"

As they walked away, Dorothy could hear them despite the other children's loud debates over who favored the best animal of all. "Six, I think," Robby said. "Sisters at Blessed Heart said five, but I know we've had birthdays since then. We might even be seven."

Eldon squatted to the boy's level, asking, "Can you take care of your business, or do you need help?"

"Help?" he scoffed, opening the door to the toilet. "Naw, I'm probably seven now that I think about it. You can go on back to the others."

Dorothy struggled to keep from laughing, especially when Eldon came back with a chagrined expression on his face. She offered, "He's probably five going on twenty-five."

He laughed. "I agree. I'd heard all about their adoption agent and journey here from Chicago from him soon after they arrived."

Mary gave a far too adult harrumph. "Some of us *know* everything, while others *say* everything. He hasn't learned to listen first and talk later."

Ralph came over to them, too. "Yeah, he might like to think he's not a baby, but he's not older than me for sure. None of us know our real birthdays. Just the ones the sisters gave us at the home."

So, her initial impressions were right. The children were orphan train riders, headed to new homes out west. "I'm sure you all are quite well behaved no matter your age. I suspect you've had to grow up fast."

"We did," Chas said. "Ma was sick before she passed, so

we learned how to cook and wash clothes for her. It wasn't enough, though."

"She died anyway," Robby offered, wiping his hands on his pants. Taking his place next to Chas, he continued. "The Sisters said God called her home. Wish He'd called us, too."

Looking into their sweet little faces, Dorothy's heart cracked into a hundred pieces. Tragedies happened out in the west like they did in the big cities. She'd taught children who'd had terrible sorrows in life. Still, when such a young child sounded so adult through misfortune, she couldn't help but want to hug and reassure them.

Instead of telling Robby he couldn't mean what he'd said and discounting his grief, she asked Eldon, "Where is their caretaker?"

"I can't tell you anything at the moment." He nodded at the children as if to indicate they were the reason why. "But later, when we're settled, we can talk more."

## CHAPTER 2

ELDON HAD NEVER FELT SO TWISTED UP INSIDE. ONE on hand, the beautiful Dorothy McLean was talking to him far more now than she ever had in all the time he'd known her. She darted into the station's post office every day to get the mail. Sometimes from him, but other times from Jerry Thompson, the station's only employee, when Eldon couldn't get there fast enough himself.

But on the other hand? When the elderly nun accompanying the current group of children west had been found dead in their railroad car? He sighed. Jerry had handled the mortician and telegraphing the orphanage but left the children's care up to him. The older man slunk off, saying Eldon was closer to their age anyway. He had to agree, but then, everyone was younger than Jerry.

Two of the children, Lucia and Juliet, were wandering

toward the bathroom. Everything distracted them on the way. Both girls stood at the window, smudging the glass as a family's wagon rolled by. Dorothy caught his attention as she walked by to them. She bent, saying something quietly. They hurried off to the restroom.

When Dorothy turned to Eldon, he smiled. Her cheeks turned pink as she returned to him, saying, "Sometimes children need reminding. Which reminds *me*. Do I have any mail today?"

"You might. I'll need to check." He hurried to the postal area as a scuffle behind the seats broke out. The rough and restless play didn't surprise him. He paused when an idea popped into his mind. "It might be a while before we hear what the orphanage wants us to do. I don't suppose you know how to keep them busy and out of trouble in here, do you?"

"I have a few things to try." She went to the children as they played tag around a bench. "Settle down, everyone, and listen to a story."

With her kind yet authoritative tone, even Eldon felt the need to obey her. He chuckled at the impulse before going to the mailroom. Nothing for Dorothy lay in the McLeans' pigeon hole, just a letter for her mother. He retrieved the message and came back to the group to find a much quieter scene. He stared in awe at her. In less than a minute, she'd had the children seated as she told them a story. She was a wonderful schoolteacher, per the town's gossip, and he'd bet anything she'd make the best mother for any man's children.

"BunBun shivered in the snow, staring into the warm home. Carrot soup cooked on the stove. His nose twitched. He could barely smell the delicious meal over the scent of humans living here."

Without interrupting Dorothy, because now he was invested in the story as well, Eldon slipped the mail to her. She didn't pause, taking the letter and placing it in her handbag. He went to sit by Ralph. The bunny's tale led to him being rescued by the people he feared, warmed, fed, and strong enough to find his way home. He stared at the young woman as she talked, unable to look away from her expressive face. Eldon enjoyed the excuse to watch her lips move. Her green eyes lit up at the children's reactions, and he loved how her cheeks turned pink when their gazes met.

Eldon lived for Dorothy's smile. The story time gave him the perfect opportunity to gape to his heart's content instead of stealing looks at her as usual. A man with more guts than him would have begun courting her by now. Eldon couldn't. He didn't know what to say to such a beauty as her. Even worse, she didn't seem to enjoy talking with him, either. She hurried into the depot, retrieved her mail, and ran out before he mustered up enough courage to say more than hello and goodbye to her.

He'd made the mistake of mentioning her to his father and sister one night at supper. Erleen latched onto the possibility of him being interested in a gal like she was a tick on the town's dog. She even lurked around to see Dorothy for herself. A lull in the story caught his attention. Dorothy frowned at him, making him realize his face also had a sour expression. He gave her a smile, motioned to continue, and resolved to ignore his sister's meddling in his life.

If Erleen needed to matchmake, she could start with their father. He'd never married after their ma died. If anyone needed a woman, it'd be Pa, considering how all the horrible meals before his sister learned how to cook, the washing, plowing, harvesting had been. Pa had done everything until Eldon and his sister were old enough to help. The man deserved some womanly care in the form of clean clothes and good food. Eldon shifted in his seat again, preferring to not ponder on anything other than the general comforts of women. Especially when he could detect Dorothy's lilac soap's scent from here. He'd dreamed of taking her in his arms and inhaling her sweet floral perfume as she nestled against him.

He shook his head, dispelling the dream. His longings could be dealt with later. Pa should marry long before Eldon, and Erleen needed to remember that. He had plenty of time to settle down. No need to rush just because his sister would soon be married to Pete. Eldon and their father could live it up as bachelors until Pa found a wife. By then, he'd want to find someone suitable, too. Someone precisely like Dorothy. She returned his grin, and he sighed, thoroughly enamored of her. Maybe even marry Dorothy instead of anyone else, if she'd have him.

"Then, when BunBun's baby bunnies grew up enough to hop to the farmer's home, he took them to meet the people who saved his life. The end."

"No!" Lucia cried. "Not the end. We need to hear more about the baby bunnies and how they ate carrot soup, too."

Tears filled Lucia's eyes, filling Eldon with panic. A crying woman, no matter what her age, terrified him. He didn't take his stare from the little girl's face as her tears began rolling down her cheeks. "Um, Dorothy? Miss McLean, I mean, don't you have more to add?"

"I might have one about her brother, um, Ralph," she said before clearing her throat. "In fact, BunBun's children all had your names and their own stories. I sadly can't tell them to you if you cry and cause a fuss or fight with each other."

The woman was a genius with children. He wanted to let her know, but the telegraph began clacking. "Excuse me, please."

Mary said, "We promise to be good if you tell us about every one of BunBun's children."

The sly tone in the girl's voice both amused and

concerned him. He'd bet anything the nuns had their hands full with that one. He sat at the telegraph, hearing Dorothy tell the group, "Very well. Since you loved the story, I plan on telling you every adventure the seven bunnies have, but it'll take some time. You'll also have to behave very well to hear everything. Can you do that for me?"

"Yes, ma'am," they replied in unison.

Eldon grinned as he focused on the telegraph machine to receive the message. The more he transcribed, the more his spirits sank. The orphanage thanked them for their telegram. Another agent would leave for Madison tomorrow. Until then, the children were to stay in the station until he arrived, with no exceptions. Eldon glanced up from the paper once the telegraph went silent. Where would they sleep in here? On the hard benches? And what about something to eat? The brief reply mentioned nothing about how to care for seven children. Jerry had to know what to do because he sure as shooting didn't. He wanted to ask Dorothy for help, but she had her school. Would she want to spend her weekend with yet another group of children?

Standing, slow and reluctant to face the group, he went around the counter to them. His stomach growled, which gave him an idea. They had to be hungry too. Fixing them a lunch would give him a chance to talk with Dorothy about the dilemma. She'd have far better ideas on what to do than he or even Jerry might. "Miss McLean? Could you help me create a meal for the children? Two hands are faster than one."

She chuckled, going to him. "You do have two, don't you?"

"Um, I mean..." he stammered, his pulse hammering with the embarrassment flooding him.

"I do know what you mean, Mr. Lukeson, and would be glad to help. Is the employees' room back there?" She nodded toward the ticket counter.

"Yes. Right this way."

She said, "Children, practice your alphabet and sums until we return," as she followed Eldon to the back.

"Aww," William hollered the loudest. "This ain't school."

"It isn't," Dorothy replied. "You're reciting for fun. See who can remember the most sums or spell the most words."

As soon as he entered the breakroom, Eldon went to the side and out of the children's sight. He motioned for Dorothy to follow him. "We need to talk."

"The telegram?" she asked. When Eldon nodded an affirmative, she grimaced. "How bad is it?"

"Bad enough that I'm not sure what to do. The new agent will be here in a couple of days, at best. The orphanage wants the children to stay here and nowhere else. We don't have places to sleep. Not comfortably, anyway."

"I see." She pulled off her gloves. "Do you have anything for them to eat here, or do I need to run to dry goods?"

"We have some stores. Not enough for several days."

"No need to worry about troubles we haven't met yet. Let's get started preparing them something to eat while you tell me everything in the telegram." She followed him as he went to the cabinet. "I have a feeling there's more and worse you've not mentioned."

He took out several apples, a chunk of cheese, and a fresh loaf of bread Jerry had brought in this morning. "You're very perceptive." Setting everything on the counter, he went for a couple of knives from the drawer. "I suppose your school teaching helps."

"It does." She took one of the knives and begin slicing the bread. "I have to be able to detect mischief when my back is turned."

Eldon grabbed the remaining knife, turning the cheese into cubes. "Can you tell what they're doing now, even from here?"

"They're arguing about something. Mainly the siblings between themselves. There's a natural rivalry between them that hasn't spread to the others yet." She took an apple, cutting it into quarters. "Give them enough time, and they'll all act as a family of seven." Taking another apple, she asked, "Where is their original guardian?"

Dang it all, he'd promised earlier to tell her and doing so had slipped his mind. Peeking out at the children to find them playing tag in the empty depot, he went back to helping cut up fruit. "She was found dead this morning in her bunk. The children don't know. Jerry told them she'd been called away. I think the older ones suspect something's wrong, but don't let on to the younger children."

"Oh goodness, how horrible. So orphaned *and* abandoned. The poor dears." She took the last apple. "If not for spring planting and the fields full of my church friends, I'd round them up to come here and help you with the orphans' care."

"I don't know. You've been doing a fine job so far."

"Thank you, but no. I know how to keep children entertained and orderly, but we'll need a real mother for them."

Instead of arguing, Eldon grasped for a reason to keep her here with him. "My ma is gone, but I have a sister. She's younger than I am and not married yet." He scratched the back of his neck for emphasis. "You're far more experienced in wrangling children than she is."

She blushed and tucked a wayward curl behind her ear. "Thank you. Teaching has helped." She stared at the clock for a few seconds before looking at him with a smile. "I do have a solution. My mother could come and help us. If you don't mind watching everyone alone, I could fetch her here."

Eldon wanted to give a war whoop at her use of "us." He tried to be calm about her considering them a team, acting like he needed a few seconds to ponder over her offer. "I suppose she'd be a good choice. Especially considering what a fine lady you are."

"I don't know about that, but I do try." She took a few steps away and toward the door. "Let me retrieve my mother while you give the children a small luncheon. You'll have all the help you'll need once she's here."

Her words worried him. He was enjoying their prolonged closeness and didn't want it to end so soon. "Will you be coming back?"

She bit her lip and nodded. "Maybe, if my mother thinks I should."

# CHAPTER 3

Dorothy rushed out of the station, breathing deep to keep from fainting. Not paying attention to anyone around her, she ran head-on into the station master, Jerry. "Oh! Sorry," she blurted. "I'm in too much of a hurry, I'm afraid."

Waving a hand, he said, "Think nothing of it, little lady. I reckon the youngsters in there have you flustered?"

She jumped on the excuse and affirmed, "Yes, that's it. They do."

"Uh-huh," he responded with a twinkle in his eye. "Has Eldon been keeping them in line?"

"Yes, very much so," she said, hoping to cast Eldon in the positive light he deserved. "I'm to find more help for him. He'll have to explain the telegram from the orphanage to you himself, however. I didn't read it."

The older man's eyebrows rose. "Word from the sisters, hmm?" He tipped his hat and opened the station's front door. "Then we'd both better get busy."

"Yes, sir." Putting on her gloves, she went home, passing by the same stores and businesses as she'd seen only a quarter or half-hour before. Yet, everything seemed different. Sparkling and crisp in the spring air because she'd talked with Eldon. Not only talked but really communicated on a far deeper level than, "Is there mail for the McLeans' here?" She bit her lip, waiting for a wagon to cross in front of her on a side street. Eldon was far more handsome when he looked at her with sparkling eyes. His warmth, the kindness toward the children, how he seemed pleased to see her every time they met. Could she love a man who she'd not spent serious time with? She didn't know but knew if any man in the world was meant for her, it'd be Eldon for sure.

Dorothy hesitated for a second at her front door. Once her mother learned of the orphans, the woman would be a whirling dervish of activity. She smiled. Junie had the same amount of derring-do as Dorothy did not. She opened the door and stepped in, hollering, "Mother, I'm home, and I have a mission for you."

Junie came over from the kitchen's direction with a hand cloth. "Darling, what's wrong that you're yelling as if this is a barn?"

She handed her mother the mail. "Sorry, but it's somewhat urgent."

A worried frown creased Junie's face. "Oh? Is your young man all right?"

Dorothy closed her eyes for a second or two as embarrassment flooded her. "He's not my young man, and he's fine." Refocusing on the dire situation at the depot, she clarified with, "It's the orphan train children who need our help."

"Orphans?" She placed the mail on the hall table. "What's happened?"

"Their elderly caretaker died while escorting them to their new homes. Now, they're to stay at the station until the new agent comes to finish the work."

She indicated their large home with a wave of her hands. "They could stay here. We have plenty of room for several children."

Smiling at her mother's first instinct of kindness for the children, Dorothy replied, "We do. Even though there are only seven left, the adoption agency insisted no one can leave the station. At least, not until their new agent arrives."

"Oh, that's not too many. I had visions of an entire train full of babies. So, we'll need to make sure they can camp there comfortably." Junie stepped toward the kitchen and hollered, "Mattie Lou, I need your assistance." She glanced at her daughter with a wry grin. "Why not yell, since we do live in a barn and all."

Dorothy laughed before crossing her arms. "See? I wasn't wrong to be so urgent."

Mattie Lou walked in, wiping her hands on a dishrag. "Yes, ma'am?"

"We're helping some orphan train children spend a night..." Junie glanced at Dorothy with raised eyebrows, who then held up a couple of fingers. "Two nights at the station," she finished. "We'll need blankets, pillows..." She looked at her daughter again. "Diapers?"

She sighed in relief at the children's post-toddler ages. "No, thank goodness. I don't know what Eldon or Mr. Thompson would do if babies were there."

Junie laughed. "I'm sure they'd manage." Back to being serious, she added, "I'll want the basket packed with enough cold foods for the rest of the day. Enough to feed how many children did you say, Dotty? Seven?"

Biting back a retort over the old nickname, she replied, "Yes, seven."

"We can completely handle seven little darlings." Junie turned to Mattie Lou with a smile. "We'll go upstairs for the bedding if you'll handle the food."

The young woman nodded, backing toward the kitchen. "Of course, ma'am."

The three women separated with Junie and Dorothy

going to the upper floor's linen armoire. She watched as her mother pawed through the various quilts and knitted blankets. Junie sighed. "I'll have to have a buggy hired to cart everything over."

She placed a thin quilt on top of a thicker one. "Or we could do this in stages. Maybe even get one of the men at the station to help?"

"I like that idea. We'll carry what we can on the first trip, then enlist some muscle for the next two or three." Junie examined the seven stacks they'd created and nodded. "Very good. Between us ladies and anyone from the station who helps us, we can finish in two trips." She picked up one of the first sets. "Shall we go?"

Dorothy followed by taking her stack too, wincing as her mother hollered Mattie Lou's name again. Really, the woman was something else. Chewing on her for yelling when she did nothing but the same.

"We'll be coming back, so don't worry about packing enough food for the entire day. Just one meal will be fine for now." Junie led them out of the front door. "Goodness, we will be a spectacle traipsing through town. Can't be helped, I suppose." She began walking to the station. Once Dorothy caught up to her, Junie asked, "Are the children very young? Or are they going to farmer families to help work?"

She ran through the orphans she'd seen. "Most of the children could be useful with small chores. They range from four to eight years old. All seem to be bright and well behaved."

"And the men at the station? How are they faring?" She paused to let a family pass by before resuming their trek. "I know Mr. Lukeson isn't a father, nor is Mr. Thompson."

Dorothy couldn't help but chuckle. "Neither was panicking, but I suspect they hovered on the verge of doing so at any moment."

Junie laughed and waved to one of her church friends across the street. "Goodness, yet again, I'm glad the children aren't babies."

Thinking of how many diapers and feedings small ones would need was overwhelming. She gave a heartfelt sigh. "So am I."

"Dorothy!" Lily hollered at them before hurrying across the street. "Aren't you a busy bee today?" Giving Junie a smile, she said, "Hello, Mrs. McLean. A pleasure to see you as always."

Not slowing down, Junie kept on to the station but returned the warm greeting to the young woman as she fell in beside them. "You too, Lily. How's your mother?"

Lily kept up, walking on the other side of Junie. "She's good. Ready to see me married off and out of her hair, she says."

"Surely not," Junie responded.

"She's teasing me, of course, saying I'm always fussing

over her, but what else could I do after her fall? She didn't break a bone, but bruising one is almost as bad, isn't it? And that doctor of hers. He doesn't prescribe anything but rest and laying around. I expected him to give her something for the horrible pain, but no. She's to just lie there and suffer. That man. We should take her to a larger city, probably Saint Louis, just to make sure she doesn't die."

When Lily took a breath, Junie jumped in. "I'm sure the doctor knows what he's doing, dear. She'll be fine in no time."

"Yes, maybe," Lily said as they went up the station's steps. She opened the door for them. "I'd feel so much better if he made daily visits and left stronger medicine is all. She cries out every time I wiggle her foot then becomes so cranky. It's terrible."

Dorothy couldn't hear her mother's reply over the children's fuss when they saw her. The seven of them ran over and began clinging to her like posters on a city lamp post. She leaned down to hug them in return. "Hello. It's good to see you all, too."

"I think they missed you," Eldon said, coming up to them. "Jerry's been threatening them with chores instead of stories.

She laughed while straightening upright. "No wonder. I'd be glad to see me as well."

Mary spoke up first. "We liked your story about BunBun."

"Yeah," William said. "You could tell us more if you want."

"Ma'am?" Eldon said to Josie over the other children clamoring for more bunny tales. "If you'd like, we have a backroom set up as the children's bedroom."

"Excellent," Josie responded. "Will you show us the way?"

"I'll help, too," Lily added, taking the picnic basket from Mattie Lou's hand. "I'd love to care for such sweet children." She rushed to catch up with Eldon. "I could help you create pallets and serve dinner to them while Mrs. McLean and Dorothy continue bringing bedding over."

He glanced over at Dorothy and talked over Lily's continued chatter. "I suppose that would be fine."

Letting the other woman hang around making eyes at Eldon was not fine at all, but what could she do? Make an embarrassing fuss? She smiled at the two of them. "Everything's ready to bring over. We shouldn't be long at all."

"Oh, no. We'll be back in a jiffy," Junie added. "Mattie Lou, I'll need to rely on you to help me plan later meals for the youngsters."

"I'll be glad to, ma'am."

Dorothy hesitated for a moment, wondering what

excuse she could create. Maybe help the children, distracted by wearing one of the empty baskets as a hat while Mary and Juliet dug the food out from the other? Or, would her, Eldon, and Lily truly be a crowd?

"Are we ready, then, ladies?" Junie asked her daughter and servant. When both nodded, she addressed Eldon and Lily. "Excuse us for now."

The three departed with Junie leading the way. Dorothy didn't mind leaving at all, not wanting to bear witness to Lily's getting to know Eldon better. Of course, he'd like the chatty woman better than he would her, she reasoned. The other woman was as animated and talkative as Dorothy was not. Lily's hair was lighter, her figure curvier, and her father not only alive but better connected in business than her own had been.

Junie's arm interlaced with hers. Giving her daughter a squeeze, she said, "Did you see the tortured look in the poor man's eyes? We'd better hurry, so he's not too trapped with her."

She frowned at her mother's smile. "Do you mean Lily? But she's so very pretty."

"Maybe so, but I think Eldon prefers another lovely young woman I know." When Dorothy gave her a side-eyed look, Junie laughed. "I completely mean you, darling. Lily might be what *you* think a man like him wants, but I'm sure he's already smitten by you."

"Smitten? Him? I..." she began but wasn't sure how to finish the sentence.

"It's all right." Junie patted her arm as Mattie Lou opened the door. "Let's get the orphans cared for and see what happens from there."

Like before, Dorothy and her mother gathered blankets and pillows enough for four children. She counted and said, "We'll need one more."

"Mattie Lou!" Junie hollered toward downstairs. "Hold off on supper. We'll need your help."

"Yes, ma'am!"

"I swear that girl has no matters." Junie divided up the last few bedclothes, creating a seventh bundle for the servant to carry. "Always making such a noise."

Dorothy chuckled. "I can't imagine where she learned such a thing, mother."

"I know, shocking." The stairs creaked as Mattie Lou joined them. "Thank you. This will only mean a slight change to your schedule."

Mattie Lou picked up a bundle and put it under her arm before picking up another to carry in the same way. "It's no bother. Once I reached the kitchen, I figured you might want me to whip up something for the children's supper, too."

"Excellent idea," Junie replied and opened the front door for the three of them. "Dorothy? Do you think Mr.

Lukeson would mind if we provided yet another meal for them?"

She followed her mother and servant outside. "I expect he'll be grateful for our help."

"I'm certain he will," Junie said with a sly grin.

Dorothy frowned but didn't argue about whose assistance Eldon would want most from the three of them. He and Lily seemed to be good friends, something she'd never dared to be with him. She shook her head as if to clear the thoughts buzzing around in there. The man could only be a post office worker to her, nothing more, and loved from afar. His interests in other young ladies in town mattered less to her than the dust on her shoes.

Except.

His smile when he saw her return a little earlier had been overshadowed by the children's greeting. Yet his pleasure at seeing her was still thrilling. They'd spoken so much together before the telegram. She'd love to continue their discussions and learn far more about him.

"Dorothy?"

She stopped and turned to look behind at her mother. Her face grew hot as she stared in shock at how she'd walked completely past the station without noticing. "Oh, goodness. I became lost in thought."

"It's all right, darling. Thank you, Mattie Lou." Junie took the bedding from the servant and held the door open for Dorothy. "Come along then. I expect you'll be greeted by another attack at any moment."

She laughed and stepped into the station. Jerry sat behind the counter, reading. Not wanting to disturb him, she led the way to the back, hearing Lily's voice echoing down the short hallway.

"I only know those stories, honest."

Dorothy bit her lip. She'd started an avalanche with her BunBun in the Snow story. Very well, she'd begun a fuss and would have to be the person to stop it. In full schoolteacher mode, she strode to the back room and entered. "What's all this, then? Don't tell me you're misbehaving."

"No, not so much as we want another story," Ralph said. "She doesn't know more than a few."

She exchanged a sympathetic look with Lily before saying, "I'm sure she told you plenty of stories." Chas and Robby came up to her, leaning against her legs. She put a hand on each of their shoulders. "Have you already eaten?"

"A tiny meal," he said. "We're still starving to death."

She glanced down at Chas, who nodded. Her intuition said they probably wanted attention more than food since Mattie Lou had packed enough for a larger group. Still, the basket seemed empty. "You poor dears. You'll all have a very substantial dinner tonight. In the meantime, let's fix your beds. Then we can have stories and playtime until time to eat."

"It's just as well because I'm going to go," Lily said, giving a wan smile to the children. "While everyone is mannerly for the most part, I have things to attend to this afternoon." She began backing up toward the door. "If Eldon comes back, tell him goodbye from me."

"He didn't say anything about returning?" Dorothy blurted. "Who'll watch after—"

"Excellent," Junie interrupted. "We'll tell him for sure." She turned to the children and Dorothy. "We can do our chores before Mr. Lukeson returns."

Lily took the opportunity to escape. Dorothy shook her head before focusing on helping her mother distribute the bedding. Spreading the blankets out with Mary, she gave the girl a reassuring smile. Lily's hinting at Eldon not coming back, leaving her and Junie here to watch the orphans didn't bother her. She wouldn't let it. If he didn't return by nightfall, she'd stay here alone for the children's sake, if necessary.

# CHAPTER 4

ELDON MADE HIS WAY BEHIND THE SEAMSTRESS'S SHOP. The narrow staircase inside led to a second-floor apartment he shared with his father and sister. More and more, he reluctantly went home every day at the end of work. With his sister at her fiancé's most of the day, their father did nearly nothing with his time. He opened the door and hollered, "Hello? Pa? Erleen?"

"She ain't here." His father shuffled into the room. "What took you so long coming back home?"

Eldon didn't want to answer and start an argument. Instead, he went over to make the beds, pushing chairs up against the kitchen table on his way. The one-room apartment was cozy in winter but already stifling in the warm spring air. He opened the heavier curtains on a north window. Finally, he decided he might as well be forthright with his father. “The orphans need a lot more care than Jerry and I were ready for. Some of the ladies in town are helping, too, but we need to give them direction.”

Mr. Lukeson pulled out a kitchen chair and sat. “Hmph. They’re ladies and know better than you or that no good Thompson does about caring for some young ’uns.”

Jerry was a good man and a friend. Every time Pa referred to him in such a dismissive way, Eldon had to choke down his anger. “Probably so, but we’re responsible for them and the building.” Wanting to change the subject and lower his irritation, he focused on his father’s needs. “Have you eaten today?”

“Naw.” Pa plopped down in a chair. “Nothing sounded good.”

Eldon paused in retrieving the frying pan from a shelf above the woodstove. “Not even coffee?”

The older man snorted. “I drank what precious little you and your sister left me.”

“All right. I can get you something.” He rummaged around for a couple of potatoes and the last quarter of an onion while the last bit of butter melted. His sister really needed to stop by the dry goods on her way home today, or he’d have to do the shopping himself. The rest of the bacon was gone, and most of the apples were mush. “Our supplies are pretty low, but we’ll have more by this evening.” He diced the lone onion, dumping the pieces into the pan. "I'll have Erleen pick us up something when she gets home today."

"Sunset is getting later all the time thanks to the longer days," his father said over the hiss of the frying food. "She won't be back in town before the store closes."

Eldon stifled an exasperated sigh. He'd forgotten about the business hours of most places. "You're right. I'll stop by and pick up a few things for us." He stirred the chopped onions so they wouldn't burn. "I don't suppose you could do the shopping for us? It'd be a real help, and you could be sure of buying everything you need."

"Naw, I'm good."

He dumped in the potato slices, biting back the retorts flooding his mind. "All right." His father sat in silence, and Eldon didn't feel like being chatty. Erleen kept far too busy at her fiancé's farm, and his postmaster duties kept him occupied as well. Since their mother's death four years ago, their father had been nearly helpless. Coaxing and threatening didn't work. The man rarely left their small apartment.

If Eldon had been paying better attention instead of grieving, he'd have visited the farm and done more for his father. Instead, he'd lived here, working at the depot and avoiding his family home until too late to save their land. Eldon regretted his cowardice. His family couldn't blame him for the loss nearly as much as he blamed himself for the negligence.

The food had appealed to him until the old memories filled his mind. Now, all he wanted to do was serve the late lunch and escape. He fixed a plate and grabbed a glass for the water. Setting the food and a fork in front of his father, Eldon said, "I'll get you something to drink, too."

"You're not eating with me?"

"No, I don't have the time today." He placed a full glass near his father. "The orphans will need to spend the night. I'll come back this evening after shopping, though, and fix you a better dinner than this."

Pa grimaced and pushed the food around on his plate with a fork. "I'd rather have Erleen cook if you don't mind. This is barely edible."

"Oh." Eldon put the pan on a cooler part of the stove before grabbing a leftover potato slice. He ate it, his stomach rumbling for more in response. "All right. I'll see if she'll cook up something tonight. I need to go."

"You're not staying to wash dishes?"

"I suppose I could." Fighting the urge to flee, he pulled a chair out and sat to wait until Pa finished. The silence stretched between them as his father ate. Uneasy at the stillness, he floundered for a safe topic. "Once the orphans are back on the train to their new homes, my schedule will be back to normal."

"What happened?" Pa asked around a mouthful of food.

Eldon stared out of the small window. Earlier today, he'd told his father what was happening at his work. He'd prefer to think of his father as uninterested in listening to him the first time instead of having anything wrong with his usually sharp memory. "The nun traveling with the children died sometime in the night." Hearing the news already seemed like weeks ago, not hours. "We've had to deal with getting her back to Chicago while caring for scared children."

"What about that schoolteacher you're always going on about? Can't you get her to take over?"

His face burned. He didn't talk about Dorothy so much, did he? His father was focused on the food, thank goodness, and not on him. He tried to use a casual tone, saying, "I could, but they're mine and Jerry's responsibility."

"Says who? Just hire her to watch the orphans until someone retrieves them."

He ignored the frustration rising in him. "Miss McLean is already watching them today while I run errands."

"Hmph." Mr. Lukeson pushed his empty plate toward Eldon. "Who's going to watch them overnight? Or are you going to lock them in and give them free run of the station?"

The idea of trapping the seven youngsters for hours in a strange and dark place horrified him. No matter how many blankets Dorothy and her mother brought them, the children would still be alone. "No, either Jerry or I will spend the night with them. They have beds already made, and the ladies are bringing them food."

"Ladies, huh?" He leaned back, his chair squeaking in protest. "Have some of them bring me dinner. I could use a little more meat on my bones."

Eldon gave him a wan smile, picking up the empty plate and dirty fork. "I can't. The children are my responsibility until the new agent arrives."

The front door opened, and like a windstorm, Erleen rushed inside. "Hello, hey, Eldon. What are you doing home so early?"

He dumped the plate and dirty frying pan into the washtub. "I might ask the same of you. Don't tell me all of your crops are planted."

"They're not." She took off her bonnet, hanging the hat on a hook next to her father's. "We're out of seed until tomorrow's shipment. Vastly annoying, so I decided to come home." She walked farther into their home. "Smells lovely in here. I don't suppose there's any left?"

"Afraid not. I need to go shopping, unless..." Eldon hinted.

"Yes, I'll go," his sister said. "We need a few things at the farm, too." She went to her father, giving his forehead a kiss. "How are you today, Papa? I left too early to say a proper goodbye this morning."

"Too early to fix me a pot of coffee, either." He gave her arm an affectionate squeeze. "I've had a headache all day."

"I'm sorry." She gave a quick glance at her brother. "We're out of beans, but they're on my list for this afternoon's shopping."

"Thank you for taking on the task," Eldon replied. "We've had a passel of orphans suddenly left at the station. I can't be gone for too long."

"Remember what I said," Pa interjected. "Get that schoolteacher to watch them. She's likely better with children than you'll ever be anyway."

Erleen chided Pa. "Father, really. Eldon is perfectly capable of wrangling a few youngsters." She winked at her brother. "As long as they're not as ornery as he was, of course."

"I don't know," he teased back, "Ma always said I was a perfect child."

"Now I'm certain your mind is gone," Erleen retorted. "Papa's right on this, though. The schoolteacher seems very capable. Why not stop by her home and see if she can help?"

"Miss McLean and her mother plus Miss Rogers already have been by a couple of times with bedding and food today."

"Oh, well, that's helpful." She looked at their father. "You seem unhappy, still, Papa."

"I am. Who's to say that gal won't be loitering around the station overnight?" He stood. "I don't like it. Women hanging around the train station, hankering for the postmaster." He pointed a finger at his son. "You need to make sure no loose woman sinks her claws into you."

Eldon ignored the urge to smart talk back to his father. "I appreciate the concern, Pa, but Miss McLean is a perfect lady at all times. She wouldn't stay at the station with me alone even if I begged her."

"Hmph, see that she doesn't. The last thing we need around here is a squalling brat whose momma runs off."

"Excuse me?" Eldon hollered at the same time Erleen shrieked, "Papa! He would never."

"Just watch yourself, young man. You'll end up at the end of some daddy's shotgun if you're not careful."

Eldon opened his mouth to argue before deciding to agree. "You're right. I'll not let any woman, no matter how mannerly, spend the night with me at the station." He grabbed a spare blanket and his pillow from his bed. "If you'll excuse me, I need to check on the orphans. I'll see you tomorrow."

## CHAPTER 5

DOROTHY SMILED AT THE OLDEST BOY. "YES, THIS IS A story about Ralph the Rabbit. I think you, in particular, will enjoy Ralph's adventures."

Ralph the boy clapped his hands. "Does he get in trouble for spitballs?"

She couldn't help but laugh at his woebegone face. "Maybe a little."

His small face sobered even more. "Will he accidentally break a window when he doesn't catch a ball in time?"

The poor child. Accidents could happen to anyone, so she reassured him. "Definitely, but not too much. He'll have to stay inside during recess and write, 'I will be careful when playing catch" twenty-five times.'

"That's not too bad." He nudged his shoulder against his sister's. "Much nicer than Sister Teresa's punishment."

She wanted to ask, even if she suspected the nun hadn't spared the rod. The children had been patient while waiting for her story, so she continued. "Ralph decided one day that the carrots his mother brought in from Farmer Dell's patch weren't as tasty as the ones he snuck from Farmer Boscoe's. Mrs. Rabbit had an agreement with Mr. Dell. She'd gather food for her small family, and he'd look the other way. Except, Ralph knew he could get away with farming Mr. Boscoe's fields for him. The old man was half lame and nearly all blind. He might have the biggest pitchfork this side of the Mississippi, but Ralph had youthful speed."

"Mr. Lukeson!" William hollered. "Come sit by me."

The other children chimed in, begging Eldon to find a seat near them, instead. Dorothy watched as he walked into the room and found a place, giving her a sheepish grin. "Sorry for the interruption. I was enjoying the story."

The warmth from his compliment seeped through her and went straight to her face. "Thank you. I'm having fun entertaining them, too."

"Ralph won't meet the business side of the pitchfork, will he?" Eldon asked.

"I hope not, but we'll have to see. Dinner should be here at any moment, so the story will have to be short."

He frowned, puzzled. "But your mother is still here."

Dorothy craned her neck toward the door, trying to see

the counter where Mr. Thompson usually sat. "What? Why?"

He shrugged, placing a begging to be held Chas on his lap. "I don't know. She's sitting behind the counter with Jerry, talking."

Her mother spending the afternoon chatting with a friend wasn't a surprise, but doing so with a man? An interesting topic which needed her full attention later. "I'm sure she'll be back in here when Mattie Lou arrives with dinner. Shall I finish Ralph's story in the meantime?"

"Yes," the children shouted. Ralph was the loudest, and Eldon added his voice, too.

She chuckled at Eldon joining in, too. "Very well. Ralph decided one day that he was tired of taking the odd carrot or two from Mr. Boscoe. Today would be when he gathered an armload of all sorts of vegetables for his mother." The children stayed quiet, intent on her every word, but Dorothy's mind wandered. Eldon seemed to be genuinely invested in the tale, increasing her shyness.

Ignoring the urge to make an excuse and flee, Dorothy instead focused on Juliet and her brother William as they listened. "Once Ralph held as many carrots, asparagus, and rhubarb as his arms could carry..." Her voice faltered at Eldon's frown. "Um, he darted for the fence but too late. Mr. Boscoe had spotted him and yelled, 'Why you pesky varmint! I'll poke so many holes in you, you'll leak when you eat soup!'"

The children laughed, and Eldon smiled. She'd have to ask him later why he seemed to disapprove of her story. An outside door closed, giving her a cue that the tale needed to finish soon. "Ralph ran and ran, vegetables dropping along the way. The farmer stabbed and stabbed, narrowly missing Ralph several times. Just as Mr. Boscoe thrust one more time, Ralph slid under the fence on his furry little tummy. He was safe."

Everyone sighed in relief, even the grown-ups. The aroma of Mattie Lou's fried vegetables seeped into the room, and Dorothy's stomach rumbled in response. "Ralph galloped at full speed all the way home." There was a frown from Eldon again. She'd have to pull him aside later for a talk about his disapproval. "He burst into the front door and gave his mother what he managed to bring. A carrot, a rhubarb, and asparagus. 'Can you make do with this, Mother?' he asked, and Mama Rabbit nodded. 'Yes, my darling, but why are you out of breath?' she asked." Dorothy stopped and shook her head. "I suppose now would be a good time for Ralph to fib, wouldn't it?"

The real Ralph nodded while every other child said, "No."

"I agree, but we know what an ornery bunny would do. Ralph said, 'I was in a race, Mother, and won.'" The children and Eldon groaned. Dorothy tried to keep a straight face and be sober. "But his mother wasn't fooled. One look at the asparagus, and she knew. 'Ralph,' she said, 'Mrs. Dell hates green vegetables. We both know you haven't been truthful to me.'"

No one in the room wore happy expressions, feeling sympathy for the punishment Ralph was sure to get. Their serious little faces tugged at Dorothy's heart. "'But,' Mrs. Rabbit added, 'you were thinking of our dinner, so I suppose I can't be too angry.'" Oh, dear, Dorothy thought, seeing the third frown on Eldon's face. His disapproval distracted her for a few seconds. She stared into his eyes, wondering where had she been in the story.

"Mrs. Rabbit should have been angry at Ralph," Mary said. "I know I would be if my brother put himself in harm's way."

In a flash, the reason for Eldon's displeasure became clear. She smiled. "Then, Mrs. Rabbit said, 'Still, you must learn a lesson that Mr. Boscoe didn't seem to teach you. No more stealing from his garden, ever. You must make me a promise.' Mrs. Rabbit took her son's hand. 'Never visit the Boscoe garden again.'"

Even Eldon leaned forward, waiting for Dorothy to give Ralph's response. She nodded, breaking the tension in the room. 'Yes, mama. I'll keep myself safe and far away from Mr. Boscoe from now on.' The end."

A cheer went up from the crowd in front of her. Clapping echoed from behind her, too. She looked to find Mr. Thompson, her mother, and Mattie Lou standing there. She bit her lip, embarrassed from their listening in on a story she'd just made up.

Junie stepped forward first. "That's a new one, isn't it, darling?"

Dorothy stood. "Yes. I thought each child might like their own bunny tale."

"Adorable idea." Junie addressed the children. "Is anyone hungry?" she asked, and when they responded with a resounding yes, she motioned toward the exit. "Then let's go eat, adults included."

"Good," Eldon said. "My stomach's been complaining since Mattie Lou first walked in."

Mattie Lou smiled. "I'm glad. The food is what I could cook fast from the root cellar."

"You've done a marvelous job, as usual." Junie led the way to the counter where the dishes were set up. "Can everyone fix their own plate, or will you need help?"

"Chas and Robby might need help, but the rest of us don't," William said. "I can take care of Juliet fine myself."

Eldon came over to Dorothy, asking, "Is there enough for them and the adults, too?"

She smiled at his eagerness and shared his hunger.

"Most likely. We didn't know if Lily or you would come back, so we had extra in case you both did."

"After smelling what Mattie Lou fixed, I'm glad," he said, taking the napkins Mattie Lou gave him to hand out to the children.

Dorothy stacked their plates. "I am, too. I figured Mr. Thompson would spend tonight with the children."

Eldon shrugged before ruffling William's hair. "He probably will, but I couldn't leave him here to wrangle them alone. I went home for my bedding to bunk down here."

"That's good," she said. "We didn't think to bring blankets for the adults to sleep on."

He shook his head before nudging her shoulder with his. "There's no need to worry. You and your family have provided enough as it is. In fact, you three might need to leave before dark, so you're not caught out at night."

She tried to focus on his words, but his touch had distracted her so. "Of course. I hadn't planned on staying much past dinner."

"Good." He waited until Chas took the plate before grabbing one for himself. "It's been nice hearing your stories but we can handle everything from here on."

"Oh." Dorothy didn't reach for her silverware, her stomach churning too much to let her eat. He didn't care for her much, after all. The frowns weren't about what she was saying as much as her in general. Now not hungry in the slightest, she managed to say, "I'm glad. We'll be leaving as soon as the children are done."

Eldon nodded, distracted by Ralph waving him over. "Good, and thank you for your help."

She watched him walk off before putting a small roll on her plate. Nothing else appealed, and she didn't even want to waste the bread but needed to make an appearance of eating around others.

"Dorothy?" Junie sat beside her. "You didn't get your food. What's wrong?"

Her eyes stung. "Nothing. I'm fine, really."

## CHAPTER 6

ELDON'S SEAT WAS COMFORTABLE AS HE SAT BETWEEN the adorable girls Lucia and Juliet while they debated about their new homes. The pale and delicate Lucia favored a place in town with puppies and kitties. Juliet, while darker but still blonde, hoped for a farm without chickens. He didn't have the heart to tell her such a thing wouldn't be possible. Everyone outside of town had at least a hen or two. Even several people in town had a small chicken coop in the alley behind their home.

"How about a baby chick? They're fuzzy like a puppy," Lucia asked the other girl.

"Yes, until it's all feathery and awful," Juliet replied, tossing a dark curl behind her shoulder. "I'll let you have the grown-up chickens to care for if you'd like."

Lucia clapped her hands. "Good. If we live close together, we'll share a puppy and a chicken."

"Except you feed one, and I'll feed the other?" Juliet asked.

"It's a deal." Lucia stuck out her hand. "Shake?"

Juliet responded with a smile, jumping up to put her empty plate with the other dirty dishes. "Yes. Let's tell the agent what we want when he arrives."

Eldon struggled to keep from chuckling at how well they'd worked out their futures. The children were well behaved so far. He glanced at Dorothy, positive she'd know when they'd stop using their best manners. He and Erleen always managed to last a week before fighting or playing a prank on their parents. With seven children, chaos couldn't be far away.

He watched as Dorothy helped the youngest children, Robby and Chas, clean their faces. Eldon loved the expressions she wore as she reacted to whatever they were telling her. He also enjoyed how no one gave him any attention. Being unnoticed left him free to stare at her as much as he wanted.

His father was wrong. Dorothy would never compromise her reputation by staying overnight with him. Fine ladies like her carefully watched how society viewed them. He fully expected the three women to take their picnic basket and go home. They'd leave him and Jerry to tend the children until breakfast, maybe even as late as lunch.

Eldon stood before going over to where the other adults had gathered, saying, "Don't forget this one." He held up the dirty plate and cutlery. Junie took the items from him as he added, "Or I'd have to pay you a visit later."

"I wouldn't mind," Junie replied. "You're welcome to come over any time."

Dorothy went behind the table Jerry had brought in, taking Eldon's dirty plate. "Although, we do keep busy enough that he'll rarely find us at home."

Frowning at her daughter, Junie said, "What? We only go out once in a while. Besides, the school year is nearly over. Both of us will be staying indoors, out of the heat this summer." She patted Eldon's arm before waving over the children. "Visit any time." To the youngsters, she added, "Who wants muffins for dessert?"

Everyone under five foot tall clamored for the sweets. Eldon stepped back to let them closer to Junie and Mattie Lou. Catching Jerry's attention, he said, "Mr. Thompson, would you keep an eye on the children while I walk the ladies home?"

"Why you and not me?" Jerry retorted.

Eldon couldn't resist teasing the man. "Because I'm younger and far more handsome."

The older man waved a hand with a smile. "Fine, go and hurry back so we can argue about your sorry opinion."

He laughed, avoiding Dorothy's gaze, and asked the other two ladies. "Are you ready, or do you need a few more minutes?"

The women exchanged a glance before Junie responded, "We can leave now without you bothering accompanying us. I'm sure you have plenty of work to catch up on before one of you goes home."

"I do," Eldon admitted, opening the door for the three women. "But I can work after the children are asleep."

"What about your bed?" Mattie Lou asked. "Do you have something comfortable to sleep on, or will you need to borrow blankets from us?

"We're rather low, aren't we?" Dorothy asked. "Although, I suppose we could pull from our beds if necessary."

"There's no need. I brought mine from home," he reassured her. Later, he'd think about wrapping himself up in her blanket, breathing her slight rose scent deep into his lungs. It'd be like holding her in his arms. Imagining her so close to him left Eldon a little dazed. Junie talked with Mattie Lou and Dorothy as they walked. Or rather Junie chatted about the latest news concerning the town, and the three of them listened. Her insights and energy drew him into agreeing with her views on what the small city needed to improve. She and his mother were similar in their concern for others. He liked Junie more with every passing minute. Giving Dorothy a side glance only confirmed what was in his heart. She might be much more subdued than her mother, but she was such a kind person. The way she cared for the children, taking over and entertaining them had only deepened his affection.

The ladies stopped in front of him, leading Eldon to almost run into them. "Oh, excuse me. I was wool-gathering."

"I figured, judging by how quiet you've been," Junie teased. "Come on, Mattie Lou. Let's clean up and get ready for tomorrow's breakfast. Dorothy, tell the young man thank you for us, will you?"

The two women were gone before Dorothy managed a squeak out a, "Yes, Ma."

"You don't have to say anything," Eldon reassured her when the door fully closed. "I was just being mannerly."

"Thank you, but I'd like to express my appreciation for your walking us home." She clasped her hands together. "You have enough to do at the station. Plus, it's not very dark out at all. We would have been fine without your escort, I'm sure."

He leaned against the porch's post with a grin. "Maybe so, but I enjoyed listening to your mother."

Dorothy chuckled. "Give it time." She took a step up

onto the porch. "I suppose I'm lucky she can do all of my talking for me."

"Surely not all," he teased. "Don't you have a few things you could say for yourself?"

"I could." She stared at her feet. "Like, I felt as if I were bothering you earlier when you first came in and said you wouldn't need our help overnight."

Eldon nodded, remembering the expression on her face, regretting hurting her feelings but unable to undo the damage his words had done. He'd let his anger at Pa show, which wasn't right at all. "I was wrong to be so blunt. Please accept my apology. You're always welcome at the station, especially if you're there to see me. I'd been overly concerned with appearances and how the town would take three lovely women spending the night with Jerry and me."

Dorothy's cheeks glowed as bright as the clouds overhead, both touched by crimson. "Oh, well, I'd been thinking of caring for the orphans more than any impropriety."

Drawn to Dorothy and her gentle nature, Eldon moved closer. The two were at eye level with her standing on the top step as he asked, "Is it improper to want to kiss you here, in public?"

"Yes, very," she whispered, staring at his lips.

He grinned, unable to resist pushing a little more

forward in his request. "Then, if I ask nicely if I could kiss you, would that ease the sting of impropriety?"

She shook her head a tiny bit. "A little, maybe, but I shouldn't let you."

Her "shouldn't" was far less of a refusal than "wouldn't," and hope blossomed in his heart. "But...you want to?"

"Yes, please." Dorothy looked into his eyes. "I can't say no."

He leaned forward, letting his lips brush hers in the briefest of caresses, but the small touch wasn't enough to satisfy him. He pushed further, deepening their contact. Dorothy gave the slightest moan, echoing the joy filling his heart. On a level deeper than he'd ever suspected, he believed she was his everything. Eldon held her close, slanting his mouth over hers, starving for more of her touch.

"What in the hell is going on here?" Mr. Lukeson stomped up the stone path.

Eldon pushed Dorothy away from him in shock from the interruption. "Nothing, Pa. We'll talk later."

"I knew it," Pa spat. "Didn't I warn you about loose women, son? But no. You've had to go kissing around on the first strumpet you found."

His father's insult and Dorothy's resulting gasp infuriated Eldon. He clenched his hands, stepping down to confront Pa. "Now see here. Miss McLean is a fine young lady who you'd be lucky to have as a daughter-in-law."

"Her?" Mr. Lukeson snorted. "This little plain dust cloth? I've never seen a more boring woman in my life. You could do better, son, much better."

The front door slammed behind Eldon. He whirled around to find Dorothy gone. Facing his father again, he ground out, "Damn, Pa, you're a mean son of a gun."

His father's right hook hit him across the jaw, knocking him on his butt. He saw stars, and his tailbone hurt. By the time he cleared his head, his father was gone. More to himself than anyone else, he growled, "You'll never do that again, or I'll make sure there's hell to pay, Pa."

## CHAPTER 7

Dorothy rushed to her room, taking the stairs two steps at a time. Flopping down on her bed, she buried her face into her pillow. What had come over her? No one ever kissed a beau in full view of the entire town. And for as long as she lived, she'd hear the strange man's voice echo in her head. Strumpet. She moaned at the memory.

If the school board found out about her? If her schoolkids' parents ever learned what she'd done tonight? If Eldon ever laughed at how the intruder had demeaned her? Dorothy felt sure she'd literally die in a puff of smoke from humiliation from any of the scenarios. She needed to pack and be on the next train out of town. Except, how could she avoid the depot and Eldon? Another moan escaped her—what a mess.

"Dorothy?" her mother called. The door creaked open. "Dearest, what's all the fuss?"

"Nothing, Mother." Her tears had coarsened her voice. "I just need some time alone, please."

The bed dipped beside her as Junie sat, placing a hand on her daughter's back. "Are you sure, darling?"

"No," she managed to reply. "I need my mother."

Junie patted her back with sharp raps. "Oh my goodness, Dorothy. You turn over this instant and tell me what happened. Did Mr. Lukeson take liberties with you? Do I need to take a swatter to his behind or alert the sheriff? Because I will."

She did as instructed, turning over, but keeping her forearm over her eyes. Doing so didn't fix anything but made her feel better nonetheless. "No. Eldon was a perfect gentleman. It was my fault I wanted him to kiss me."

"Oh. I see." Junie's silence stretched out for nearly a minute before she asked, "And did he kiss you?"

Shame roiled in her gut as she confessed, "Uh-huh."

Junie sighed before another long quiet. "Did you care for it?"

"Very much so," she admitted, unable to lie to her mother.

"Did he seem to enjoy the kiss, too?"

Remembering how Eldon's lips felt against hers, soft yet firm, and gentle but insistent, left her heart melting for him all over again. She sat up, facing her mother. "Yes, I'm sure he did."

Junie smiled, smoothing her daughter's loosened hair from her face. "I don't see the problem then."

Fresh tears sprang to Dorothy's eyes at the memory of what happened next. "We were interrupted by some angry man who called me a strumpet." To her dismay, her voice cracked on the last word. "I'm not some loose floozy."

"Not at all, darling," Junie said in a soft voice, taking her daughter in her arms as Dorothy sobbed. After a few seconds, she asked, "Do you know who the man is?"

She sniffed. Her mother's angry voice was so sharp, it could cut the hardest stone. "I think he's related to Eldon. He looks like an older, meaner, and rottener version of him."

"Well, then. I'll have to give Eldon a visit tomorrow and ask about his father."

The fantasy of Junie chewing the man up one side and down the other held a certain appeal, but wouldn't take away what he'd said. She shook her head, reaching for a handkerchief from her nightstand. "I'd prefer you didn't. I think Eldon is as embarrassed as I am by the entire debacle. He probably wants to never see me again as much as I never want to see him, either." The idea of him disliking her broke her heart anew, and she began sobbing.

"There there, darling." Junie comforted her with a hug.

"I know your first kiss was interrupted, and the horrible man said horrible things. But you're nothing close to a strumpet. I'll bet my last penny Eldon knows you're a wonderful young lady."

"I hope so," Dorothy whispered.

Junie let go and stood. "When you come with Mattie Lou and me to give the children their breakfast, you can talk everything over with Eldon. Clear the air and start fresh."

She lay back down, shaking her head. "No."

"No?" Junie put her hands on her hips. "Whyever not?"

"I can't face him after this." Dorothy rolled back over on her stomach to ease the ache. "I refuse to ever see him again. Ever."

## CHAPTER 8

RAGE FILLED ELDON SO MUCH HE COULDN'T BREATHE. Going home to confront his father would merely end in a horrible fight. He turned in the opposite direction and began walking. One of the most beautiful moments in his life until now had been ruined thanks to Pa's horrible temper and foul words. He nodded at someone familiar as he approached and returned to a scowl once the gentleman had passed. Most of the town was closed for the day. His steps on the boardwalk rang out hollowly, only fading as he approached and then passed the saloon. A drink might take the edge off his anger, but he needed to return to the station. Jerry had three grown children and several grandchildren. If anyone could wrangle seven youngsters, he'd be the man to call.

Eldon turned around to head home before going to the

station. The walk back would give him time to think about Dorothy anyway. Everything in his life fell in place the instant their lips met. He wanted to spend the rest of his life with her. While he wasn't sure how, where, or when, Eldon knew in his heart, she was his future wife.

Now, all Eldon had to do was convince her *and* his father. He shook his head and paused in front of the seamstress's shop. Even if Pa never accepted Dorothy or any woman as his wife, he didn't care. Pa had found Ma and love. He figured he had the right to do the same.

Eldon went around to the back and climbed the steps to the second story. After a couple of knocks, he went in. Erleen stood up. "You just missed dinner. We thought you'd be at the station."

"I went for a walk to think about things," he responded. "I'm not hungry, anyway." He pulled a chair out and sat, facing his father. "I'd like to talk to you about this evening and what happened."

Mr. Lukeson glanced up from his book with a glare before standing and leaving the apartment without a word. Eldon looked over at his sister. "Did he say anything to you?"

Erleen put a plate with meat and a slice of bread in front of him. "Yes, and none of it was good. You were kissing a woman in public tonight?"

Irritation at the implication Dorothy was an ordinary

lady rushed through him, and he countered with, "Not a woman but *the* woman. The one I want to marry."

Erleen frowned. "She's not a girl for hire?"

He gripped the fork so hard his fingers hurt as he growled, "She's the schoolteacher, Miss McLean."

His sister snorted. "Dowdy Dotty McLean? But she's so quiet and plain. I know so many other ladies who pester me about you all of the time."

Eldon didn't care about anyone else. Dorothy was the only lady on his mind. "She's not flashy, no, but she's a kind, sweet, and mannerly young woman. I like the way she looks at me as much as I do her gentle beauty."

Erleen propped her chin up, resting her elbow on the table. "It's love, then."

He nodded, his neck stiff from all his pent-up tension. "It is, and all I have to do is convince Dorothy."

Shrugging, Erleen said, "Just tell her how you feel. Be honest, and she can't help but return your affections."

He took a bite of the dinner. The taste left his stomach growling for more. After a swallow, he asked, "Do you think Pa will ever like her?"

"Pa won't be the one marrying her, so it doesn't matter what he thinks."

He took another bite, eating without tasting. Was he ready to commit his life? Memories of how Dorothy's lips met his, how she clung to them as they kissed and knew without a doubt. "You're right. If she'd have me, I'd marry her tomorrow."

Erleen laughed. "Congratulations. Should we plan a double wedding?"

He rolled his eyes at how much her opinion had changed so soon. "Let me propose to her first."

She came over to him, taking the empty plate and giving him a hug. "She'll say yes. How could she resist such a wonderful man?"

"You'd be surprised." He stood, stretching. "Thank you for the meal. I didn't know I was hungry."

"Do you have to go to the station right away?" Erleen asked with a sly tone. "Could you visit Dorothy first?"

Curious about her ulterior motives, he said, "I hadn't planned on seeing her until tomorrow."

"Maybe give her a brief apology for Pa's actions?" she countered.

The idea was sound. Plus, the more Eldon thought about it, the more he wanted to see Dorothy again. "Yes, I'll stop by, apologize, and then go to help Jerry with the children."

"Good," Erleen said, giving him a quick hug. "Take care, and don't worry. Pa will come around to accepting her eventually."

Eldon nodded, not trusting his voice at the moment. He left the apartment, sure he had the best sister in the world.

She'd helped him clarify what he wanted for his future. Their father wasn't on the stairs or outside. The night had grown cooler since Eldon had gone indoors. A shiver went through his body. Stars shone down on the town, unhampered by any moon. He reached the front of the building and first looked right, then left. One way led to the station. The other led to Dorothy's home.

He had to see her and apologize before doing anything else. Pulled to her as if they were linked by a rope, he went to the McLeans' home. Everything he wanted to say jumbled around in his mind like popping corn on a campfire. Would she accept his apology or still be furious?

Too soon, Eldon stood on her front step. He moved closer, wondering who would answer, what would they say? The only way he could be sure was to knock on her door. He stepped forward, raised his hand, and tapped.

No answer. He waited a few seconds before tapping again.

Still no answer. His heart in his throat, he rapped harder on the thick wood. He heard a few squeaks as if someone was running downstairs. His mind blanked. He stepped back, fighting the urge to run before the door opened.

Junie appeared, frowning at him at first before her face relaxed into a smile. "Yes? Oh, Eldon, what are you doing out this time of the evening?" She peered around him. "Are you alone, or is that dreadful man with you?"

So she knew about what Pa had said, but had she learned of the kiss? Eldon didn't want to know for sure, or he'd lose his nerve. "No, my father is at home. May I speak to Dorothy for a moment? I'd like to apologize for earlier."

"Oh, dear. Your father, hmm? I'm sorry for calling him dreadful." Junie bit her lip like he'd seen Dorothy sometimes do. "I'm sure he's a fine man in other circumstances."

"And Dorothy?" he pressed. "May I say a few words to her?"

Junie shook her head, closing the door halfway. "I'm afraid not. She's quite upset, and after what was said this evening, I can't blame her."

To be so close to the love of his life, yet she refused his apology? Eldon's heart cracked in two. "Please, Mrs. McLean, let me see her for just a minute. I'll explain everything. Tell her she's not at fault, and my father was horribly mistaken."

"It's not my choice, dear boy, but hers." Junie reached out for his shoulders and turned him around. "Leave for now. I'll talk to her tomorrow and try to change her mind. If you persist tonight, you'll only make her hate you."

## CHAPTER 9

DOROTHY HELD HER BREATH FOR A FEW SECONDS before following her mother into the station. A crowd of people fresh from the latest train kept her distracted from looking for Eldon as she wove in among them.

There. At the counter sorting mail. As if possessed with a supernatural sense of knowing she had arrived, Eldon looked up from his work. Their gazes met, and her heart stopped. He was so very handsome. Kind, too, and it hurt to look away first. She tapped her mother on the arm. "I need to go outside. Can you serve breakfast to the children alone?"

"Yes, darling, of course I can." She put her free arm around Dorothy. "Come back when you feel more comfortable."

"Thank you, Mama." She turned on her heel, filing out

with the leaving passengers. Once free of the station, she took a deep breath in relief. No matter how much she adored Eldon, she couldn't accept a man with a father like his.

She paced in front. Her heart wanted Eldon to come out and kiss her again. Her mind, though? Her far more rational part dreaded his pursual. She walked a little farther down the station's boardwalk. He'd been so desperate to talk to her last night, too. She had gripped her hands into fists on the stair's guardrail to keep from running down and jumping into his arms. But his father calling her a strumpet echoed in her mind before she took the first step towards him. No. She was doing the right thing in avoiding all of the Lukesons—every last one of them.

"Miss McLean? Why aren't you telling us a story?"

Oh no. Lucia was next on her bunny tale list. The little girl with her golden hair and china-blue eyes had Dorothy wrapped around her finger with every smile. "You're right. I should be telling you all about Lucia Bunny and the surly toad." She took the child's hand. "Let's go inside, and I'll tell the story while you finish breakfast."

"Yay!" she cried and swung her arm in glee.

Dorothy opened the heavy station door to find Eldon standing there. A mean thought came to mind, and she blurted, "Did you send Lucia in after me?"

"No, but I did tell her where you were when she asked."

The wind taken from her angry sails, she lost all of her blusters. "Oh, thank-you. It seems I owe them a few more stories before they leave for the new homes."

"I figured as much. The children are done with breakfast, judging by the noise."

"Thank you." Shy from the kindness in his eyes, Dorothy hurried to the side room full of children. The poor darlings all looked worse for wear. Their clothes had been slept in. Juliet's messy face told Dorothy exactly how good Junie's preserves had been. William had his shirt off and was using the garment to play tug of war with Ralph. The rest of the children were throwing dinner rolls at each other. "Mary, Lucia, Robby, and Chas, pick up every one of those rolls this instant or no more stories." As the children rushed to mind her, Dorothy hurried over to the washroom, finding Junie there. "Mother, they're acting so horribly. Why didn't you come to find me?"

"And make you face Eldon when you weren't ready?" She wiped her hands on a towel before dipping a corner in water. "I couldn't. Why are you in here, anyway?"

"Lucia wants her story," she admitted, the excuse sounding thin to her when said aloud.

"Ah, I don't blame her." Junie went into the children's room. "Your entertaining them will give me the chance to clean up breakfast without too much of a fuss." She frowned. "William, you'll tear up your shirt. Put it back on this instant. Ralph, let go now." She went over to Juliet, wiping the young girl's face.

Dorothy hid a smile. She might be shyer than her mother, but in a classroom, she was every bit as bossy as Junie was. "Come along, everyone. If you want to hear the tale of Lucia Bunny and the Angry Toad, gather around and keep still."

They did as she requested. Even rumpled, the seven of them were adorable. Mary and Juliet sat with Lucia in between them. Ralph and William flanked the girls on one side, Robby and Chas sat on the other. Her mother began cleaning up the plates and cutlery as a story came to Dorothy's mind.

"Once upon a time, a princess bunny named Lucia lived in a forest with her other bunny friends. She played and hopped in the meadows with them every day. They'd nibble on grass, playing hide and seek, and get drinks from a shallow creek in the valley. Everything was lovely until one day, Lucia hopped on a toad's toe. This toad hollered and screamed, rolled and failed, croaked, and cried for several minutes. Lucia tried apologizing..."

A little splinter of guilt embedded in her conscience. Eldon had tried, too, but she'd turned him away. Was she an angry toad? Surely not. "She tried more than once, yet the toad was too upset to listen." Dorothy desperately wanted to move on from the subject, especially when seeing the sly grin on her mother's face. "So she continued on, getting a sip of clean water from the creek. Hopping back to her friends, she had to pass the angry toad again."

Oh dear, this wasn't working out at all. How could Dorothy stop talking about the toad, and Eldon by proxy, when he was such a part of the story? She tried smiling as the children fidgeted. "Hop. Hop. Hop. Lucia edged ever closer to her enemy, hoping he didn't notice her. Hop and oh no! The angry toad saw her. He ran up to Lucia and demanded, 'Where's my apology? Where's your sorry?'" Dorothy shook her head. "But Lucia didn't say a word. If what she'd offered wasn't good enough then, it wouldn't be good enough now. She hopped on, hop, hop, hop, and the toad followed, complaining all the way."

Her mother paused her folding of a tablecloth for a second before resuming her work. Something had distracted her, and before Dorothy could wonder why, she heard a masculine throat clear behind her. "Excuse me? I hate to interrupt, but I have news about the adoption agent."

Dorothy turned to face him. "No need to apologize for important information." A few giggles came from behind her, and she blushed, sure they were thinking of the angry toad.

"Good, because I'd hate for my apology to go unaccepted." He straightened. "At any rate, we received a telegram just now. The orphanage has sent for an agent from Saint Louis instead of Chicago. They're due to arrive late this afternoon. I'd recommend everyone behave better so they can listen to all of the bunny tales before they leave." He grinned at Dorothy. "Talk fast, and I'll let you know when the agent gets here."

"Thank you, Mr. Lukeson." She faced the children again. "Well, that's good news. You'll see your new parents sooner than we expected." They began talking among themselves, brothers and sisters moving to sit next to each other.

Lucia came up to Dorothy and sat on her lap. "Do you think my parents will like me?"

"I'm sure they will," she replied, and the girl hugged her. "Does everyone want me to finish the story, or should we take a break?"

"Story first," Lucia said.

"Yes, a story first because mine is next," William added.

Dorothy laughed and let Lucia slide to the floor. The girl scrambled into place between Juliet and Mary. "Where was I? Ah, yes, the angry toad began following Lucia Bunny to where her friends waited for her."

Juliet raised her hand. "Excuse me, Miss McLean? I know a secret."

She smiled, not bothered by the sudden interruption, thanks to a need to rethink the angry toad's role. "What's that, darling?"

"Mr. Lukeson is sweet on you."

Horror filled her. Were their affections so obvious? Did Dorothy wear a sign saying, "Has been kissed by a man" around her neck? She stammered, "What? No, Mr. Lukeson is just a kind man is all."

Mary snorted. "He is, but he makes calf eyes at you."

William laughed and nudged Ralph. "Yeah, he's sweet on you, ain't he?"

"Oh, pshaw," she said, trying to brush away the topic. "No matter what he thinks of me, it doesn't matter. Let's get back to the story."

"Why, Miss McLean?" Juliet asked, her voice ringing out through the room like a church bell. "Aren't you sweet on Mr. Lukeson, too?"

"I..." Dorothy began, not wanting to lie, but not quite willing to give the truth. "I do like him. He's a very kind man." She straightened. "Now, then, let's finish the story before the agent arrives, shall we?"

# CHAPTER 10

ELDON FIGURED HE GOT WHAT HE DESERVED. Eavesdroppers always did. He turned away, his jaw clenched, and headed for the mailroom. Their momentous kiss meant little to her.

As he took a couple of steps past the counter to his mailroom, Jerry piped up. "Not staying for the rest of the story?"

He frowned and struggled to keep from snapping at his friend. "You can hear her from here?"

Jerry chuckled. "Sure, a little. I keep my ears clean."

Resisting the urge to reply with a sharp retort matching his comment, Eldon paused, unsure of how much to confide in the older man. "It's just a story about a rabbit and a frog for children."

"Maybe so, but it's the most entertaining thing we've

had happen here in months. I mean, all the children are." He went back to reading his paper. "Other than her coming in for the mail and you two getting all moony-eyed over each other, that is."

His mind blanked for a few seconds, shocked that he'd been so obvious. "We don't."

Jerry glanced up for a brief second. "Don't you? Hmph." He shook his head. "Even the orphans noticed your feelings for each other."

Eldon went over to him, closer to talk without anyone else hearing. "I'm not the only one, then? She looks at me all goofy, too?"

Jerry chuckled. "Absolutely. I don't know what happened in the past few days to leave her shyer than usual, but she didn't change her mind about you much."

Much? He might as well confess everything since Jerry seemed to know everything going on around here. "If you must know..." he began, and Jerry pushed aside his paper to listen. "Last night, my father threw a fit when he saw Dorothy and I kiss outside of her home. She turned tail and ran, wouldn't answer the door when I came back later to apologize."

Understanding broke across the older man's face. "Ah, is she avoiding you for the kiss or for your pa?"

The question surprised him. Had Dorothy suspected

he'd want to take back the kiss they had shared? "I don't rightly know, now that you ask."

Jerry shook his head and picked up his newspaper. "Women think differently than we do. She might have been afraid your pa forced you to give her a retraction on the smooch."

Eldon could think about the mishmash of Jerry's high falutin' words mixed in with his more primitive ones later. "You might be right. I'll have to think about how I want to fix this while I'm sorting mail."

The older man chuckled. "If you need any help in thinking, holler. I'm pretty good at saying sorry to pretty girls."

The idea of Jerry being in trouble with the ladies amused Eldon into a slight smile despite his blues. "I will."

"You'd better. Just because I'm between wives doesn't mean I'm ignorant about the ladies," he kidded.

Eldon couldn't help but laugh outright. "You're the first person I'll ask for help, then." Without waiting for a snappy retort, he went to the mailroom. Only two bags waited for him from the morning train, and the westbound stage from Saint Louis was due at any moment. He figured he could be halfway through by the time it arrived.

Sure enough, he'd finished one bag and had the next one opened when the front door slammed shut. A handful of letters or so could be sorted by the time the coach boy made his way back to him.

"Where are they?" a gruff-voiced woman asked outside of the mailroom. "I need to see if they're well."

Eldon glanced up at the question. A lady in a nun's habit asking about children could only mean the orphans. He stopped what he was doing and went to join Jerry as the man replied, "I reckon you're the adoption agent we've been told to expect?"

The older woman made Jerry look younger and far less cranky as she growled, "Sister Agatha from Blessed Heart. I just arrived on the stagecoach and am not feeling like playing games. Where are they?"

From his side vision, he saw Dorothy in the children's room doorway with the crowd of orphans around her. The front door shut again as Junie and Mattie Lou walked in with a basket of food. Eldon crooked his head in Dorothy's direction, and replied, "The children are in a separate room being cared for by a local schoolteacher. I'll take you to them."

The older woman wrinkled her nose. She stomped past him as the children came over to the adults. "No need. I can see them just fine. Where are their belongings?"

Eldon called after her, "They didn't arrive with any."

She stopped and whirled around to face him. "What? You didn't unload their baggage from the train? What nincompoop didn't think to provide these children with their own clothes." She marched over to Mary, picked up a braid, and sniffed. "Good Lord almighty have mercy." Frowning at Dorothy, she said, "Some care you've provided. These children are filthy. I'll have to take extra time making sure they're clean for their new families and retrieve their work clothes from wherever they've ended up." Grumbling, she inspected each child's hands. "Clean. Good. At least you've done this much. Have they eaten their midday meal yet?"

Dorothy glanced at her mother and Mattie Lou before admitting, "Not yet. Their food is in the baskets."

Sister Agatha glared at the three women. "I see, so you have been feeding them?" After the trio nodded a response, the nun strode over to the pallets. "The bedding is thin, but the air is warm enough in here. Who stayed with them last night?"

"We did," Eldon offered. "Me and Mist—"

"Don't tell me you and this young lady," the nun hollered. "Unless you two are married, you two have no business caring for children together."

Junie went to stand by her daughter. "Excuse me, but a woman of God or not, you need to know Dorothy was with me all evening. Nothing improper happened, and you might want to refrain from unfounded conclusions."

Eldon nodded, unable to keep from chiming in. "We

were fortunate, Mister Thompson and I, in having Miss McLean and her family's assistance. Believe it or not, this is a working train station, not a hotel. Mrs. and Miss McLean have been nothing but kind to the children."

The woman looked at each one of them. She peered as if trying to see through their skin and into their souls. At last, she snorted. "Very well. I'm sure nothing improper happened, even if the circumstances were less than ideal. Who operates the telegraph around here? I'll want to send a telegram to the agency about the children's status and take them with me on to Kansas City to their families."

"What about our bunny tales?" Juliet asked. "I'm next, and I want my story."

"I don't know anything about stories, young lady," the nun answered.

"Excuse me, but I do, Sister," Dorothy offered. "I'd been telling them tales about bunnies to keep them amused while we waited for you, one for each child."

"Oh." She looked from one orphan to the next. "How many are left?"

"Three," Dorothy replied.

"Do they take long?" the sister barked.

"No," she said.

The nun heaved a massive put upon sigh. "Very well. Tell them over dinner and until we board the train afterward." She turned to Junie and Mattie Lou. "I assume you'll serve the meal?"

"We will," Junie replied. "And have plenty for the adults, too."

"Ah, an unexpected treat." She ruffled Chas's hair before smoothing it back into place despite the cowlick. "Any sort of eating on the stage is difficult. Plus, I'll enjoy sitting on a stable seat."

Eldon heard the front door opening, and the familiar plop of a mailbag from the stagecoach echoed through the large room. He had to grin at the delay between the nun and the mail arriving here. The agent must have shoved people and carriages out of her way in a rush to see the children.

Just as he was about to go back to sorting mail, Juliet said, "When you tell my story, Miss McLean, can Mr. Lukeson listen too?"

"Certainly, he can, if he's not too busy," Dorothy replied.

The children giggled before Mary said, "A man is never too busy for his sweetheart."

The nun whirled around, plate in hand. "What?"

"Miss McLean and Mr. Lukeson are sweethearts," Robby offered.

"Yeah," Juliet added. "We talked about their calf eyes earlier."

Sister Agatha glared at Dorothy first, then Eldon. "You discussed a romantic relationship with the children?"

"No," Dorothy squeaked. "They mentioned one, but we both dismissed the idea."

More giggles erupted from the children before William began chanting, "Calf eyes, calf eyes, we see their calf eyes."

Eldon almost laughed before seeing Dorothy's dark blush and the nun's fury. He stepped forward and raised his hands to quiet them. "Everyone, neither of us are sweet on each other one bit. Settle down and let's have dinner."

"There's no let's about this," Sister Agatha roared. She pointed toward the door. "Mr. Lukeson, I suggest you go back to work, and Miss McLean, thank you, but your services are no longer needed. Clearly, there have been improprieties happening, and it's best if the adults leave. You may retrieve the dishes and bedding after we're gone, thank you."

# CHAPTER 11

A BLISTERING WAVE OF EMBARRASSMENT SWEPT through Dorothy. No one in the room seemed to breathe in the heavy silence. She nodded, mortified at the spectacle the Godly woman made in front of everyone. "Very well. I'll leave." Going to Mary first, she hugged the stunned girl as Robby and Chas came over to cling to her skirts.

Before she could say the rest of her goodbyes properly, Eldon spoke up. "Sister Agatha, I realize you need to enforce propriety among the children's caregivers, but you've gone too far. Miss McLean is a fine young woman, no matter how many people malign her."

"Yes, she is, and he's right," Junie added. "My daughter has been nothing but joy in everyone's life, including the children's. I'd suggest you rethink your harsh words."

Dorothy snuck a glance at the stern sister. The woman's

gaze didn't waver from its intense stare at Eldon as she said, "Mr. Lukeson, many people? Who else sees a problem with Miss McLean's reputation besides me?"

"Umm, no one. No one does," Eldon stammered. "Everyone in town thinks her behavior is impeccable."

She bit her lip in dismay. One of Eldon's best qualities was how horrible of a liar he was. The way his ears flushed when he fibbed would be adorable at any other time. William came up to her, too, putting his arms around her and Mary both.

"Bearing false witness is a sin and one you need to repent," the nun said and raised her hand. "I don't have time for this. I'll not apologize for telling the truth, and all the adults can leave now. Say your goodbyes, children, and let's clean up for the next train to your new families." Lucia began crying, and Mary put an arm around her. The nun frowned. "Tut tut, stop that this instant. She's merely going home as you will be soon." Still scowling, she addressed Dorothy, "Go, before this becomes even messier."

Dorothy didn't want to admit the sour woman was right but had to agree. Drawing out the farewell would upset the children more than they already were. "One of the men can let us know when to pick up the dishes and bedding later." She gave each of them a squeezy hug, saying their name with affection. "Mary, William, Robby, Juliet, Lucia, Ralph, and Chas. I'm sure you'll all be as good as possible for your new families."

"We will," Ralph said, not letting go of her while Chas clung to her. "But who'll tell us the rest of your stories?"

Her eyes stung with unshed tears as she kneeled to their level. "Well, I'll need to count on the older children to tell the adventures of Juliet Bunny, Robby Rabbit, and Chas Hare. I have faith in all of you and in your abilities to create a wonderful future for yourselves." She held them for a few seconds as Sister Agatha shifted from one foot to the other with a sigh. Irritated at the woman's mean impatience, Dorothy stood. "One last hug." Robby joined his brother in crying, and even Mary's eyes filled with tears. "Now, now. You're all just hungry. Have your dinner and tell your stories."

Dorothy pulled away from the younger children reluctantly. She debated on talking back to Sister Agatha and refusing to go. But, the example she'd set would be a bad one, so she held her head up and left the room. Tears spilled down her face as she fled the station with Junie and Mattie Lou behind her.

# CHAPTER 12

Eldon used every ounce of his self-control to stay in place and let Dorothy leave the depot. The front door slammed shut when the three women exited the building. Sister Agatha was already ordering the children around, telling them to eat, clean up, and be ready when their train pulled into the station.

"Don't you have work to do, young man?" the nun asked him.

He looked at her, struggling to keep his voice quiet. "Not only is Miss McLean a fine and decent woman, if I'm lucky, she'll also agree to marry me someday."

"Fine and decent young women don't have reputations." She pointed a bony finger at him. "You'd be better served by finding your wife in church instead of a train station. Nothing good can come from meeting a woman here."

He glared at her. "Are you telling me only ungodly women ride the train?"

The question took her aback. "I, well, no. Most of our agents travel via railroad." She crossed her arms. "None of them loiter around, looking for trouble once they disembark."

He wanted to shake sense into the woman but kept his hands clenched. "Miss McLean is always polite and circumspect when she picks up her family's mail, as is every single lady in town." Eldon stepped forward as Sister Agatha stepped back. "My father has a good reason for my not marrying Miss McLean. He'll be alone once I have a new home, but you? You have no reason to malign someone kind and innocent like her. Since you're incapable of remorse, our conversation is finished."

Eldon turned before Sister Agatha could recover from his onslaught. He didn't run to his mailroom to hide so much as hurried back to work. At least, he ignored the urge to flee the harpy. Guilt filled him when he saw the three-person line queued up for the mail office. "Sorry. I had a few things to finish up with some Orphan Train riders." He went behind his counter and faced Lily Rogers first. "How can I help you?"

"I'd like to mail a letter back east to my cousin plus see if I have mail from her yet."

"Let's see." He rushed to check the Rogers' box but found it empty. "Nothing yet, but I have a fresh bag in from the afternoon stage." He went back to the counter, accepting the letter she wanted to send. "If there is something for your family, I can bring it by after I close up for the day."

"Would you? That would be so helpful."

"Certainly. If I'm not there by dark, you all didn't get anything today." He stamped her envelope with a postmark. "That'll be ten cents, please."

She dug around in her coin purse. "So expensive." Digging deeper, she asked, "I don't suppose you could only charge me five cents?"

He shrugged. "I could, but your letter would end up in Kentucky somewhere."

"All right," she grumbled. "Ten cents it is."

He smiled, sliding the coin into the change drawer and writing out a receipt. Lily said the same thing every time she bought a stamp, giving him a chance to invent a witty retort every time. "Have a good afternoon."

"I should since my purse is so much lighter now."

Eldon laughed and waved her on. The next person stepped up, the head of the town's only bank. "Good afternoon, how may I help you?"

"I have a letter to mail. It might take more than ten cents."

He examined the address and put a postmark on the envelope. "No, ten pennies even if it is going to Maine. Like I mentioned to Miss Rogers, if I see a letter to you while sorting the incoming mail this afternoon, I'll deliver it to your home."

"Oh, no, there's no need to do that," the dandy man replied. "I can pick it up tomorrow at noon or so. I enjoy walking over here sometimes. Clears my head, you know, the fresh air and all."

He had a point, Eldon admitted, so he replied, "I understand, and anything you receive will be waiting for you when you're ready."

"Thank you." The banker nodded and hurried away.

Eldon noticed even the back of the man's neck was red with embarrassment and smiled. Judging by the lovely cursive and slightly sweet scent on the letters from Maine, he could imagine why the banker might blush.

"I never received my Wish Book."

A lady not much older than Junie McLean stood in front of him. He gave her a smile, confessing, "Ah, Mrs. Murphy. I was wondering when you'd notice." He went to Murphy's mailbox and retrieved the Montgomery Ward's latest catalog. "Your husband said you didn't need it."

"That rascal." She took the magazine from him. "He

says that to keep me from knowing the latest products." She leaned against the counter, flipping through the pages. "Curses up a blue streak when I buy anything but enjoys the results just the same. New blankets, the finest perfume, a tin of salmon are all fine once I've ordered them, but mention I'm going to purchase anything and he's so cranky."

Eldon laughed. "I'll remind him good things come from the Wish Book, too, the next time he tells me what to do with it."

Her jaw dropped for a moment before she recovered. "I hope Murph isn't too rude."

"Not too much," he admitted with a grin.

She shook her head, wandering off toward the door while muttering, "That man. I swear I'll never get him raised..."

In a better mood, thanks to his customers, Eldon went to the mailbag and began sorting. The task didn't take long despite the few lost letters. He put them in the box under the counter and looked out over the depot. This time of day, mid-afternoon, the station was quiet. He expected noise from where the children were but heard nothing. A little concerned, he left his area, nodding at Jerry when the other man looked up.

Once in the doorway, he saw the reason for the quiet. All of the children were napping. Each had their own pallet, and Sister Agatha? She was in a chair, leaned back, her mouth agape as she slept. He frowned. At least, he hoped she was asleep. Watching her chest, he relaxed when seeing her breathe. Thank God. The last thing he wanted was to have another trip to the morgue.

The dirty dishes were stacked in the picnic baskets. Work was caught up, and most people didn't stop by for mail this late on a Saturday. He picked up the baskets, bringing them into the main room. "Jerry, I'm taking these to the McLeans' and will be right back if anyone needs me."

"Good luck, and say hello to Mrs. McLean for me."

"Thank you, and I will." Eldon walked out and ran into his sister and her fiancé. "Erleen, Pete, good to see you."

"Eldon," Pete said, tipping his hat.

"We're here to pick up a few things for Pa and to talk to you," she said.

He didn't feel like being in a conciliatory mood. "Oh? Has he apologized for what he said to Dorothy?"

"No, but I think he feels bad." She dragged her toe back and forth in the dust covering the boardwalk. "He said something about asking if you'd mentioned anything more about her to me."

His hackles rose. "What did you say?"

She glanced at Pete before saying, "I told him you'd not said anything to me. Which you hadn't."

Eldon nodded. "It's true. I've been busy."

"I don't want to interfere," Erleen began, "but you might make time for Dorothy soon and apologize for Pa. I'm sure he'll soften and see how wrong he was. Tell her how you feel."

"I already have," he admitted.

Erleen took his arm, shaking him a little. "Tell her again. Make her believe you. She's the only woman you've ever talked about as if you cared deeply for her. We don't live in a large city, you know. She might be your only chance, and you don't want to end up like Pa, bitter, and alone."

He didn't want to say anything more in such a public place, so Eldon raised the baskets a little. "I have a good reason to talk to her. I'll meet you back at Pa's later?"

"Yes, and don't forget a single word she says to you. I want to hear everything that happened." She gave him a quick but awkward hug before pulling Pete with her.

Eldon continued on. Dorothy's home wasn't as close to the station as he'd hoped, given the heavy dishes. He had a new respect for Junie's and Mattie Lou's strength. While not a weak man, pausing to talk had reminded him of how easy his work was.

He stopped in front of the McLeans', glad to have more of an excuse to visit than to pine away for Dorothy. He knocked on the door, fighting the urge to dump the baskets there and hurry back to the station.

The door opened, and Junie stood there. "Hello, and thank you for coming." She reached for the baskets.

"No, ma'am, I'll carry them in for you." He stepped in when she moved back. "You should have had Jerry and me cart these back and forth for you all."

"Maybe so," she admitted with a chuckle, leading him down the hall and into the kitchen. "I'll admit I enjoyed setting them down finally."

He looked around the house, enjoying how much of a real home it was. "If it's not too unmanly of me, I'm looking forward to being done with them, too."

Junie laughed, taking one of the baskets from him as he sat down the other. "Be glad the children ate the food and lightened your load."

He stared at her with new respect. For all of her easygoing chatter and bluster, Junie McLean was a strong woman. "Now that you mention it, I am."

"You didn't eat lunch, though, did you?" she smoothly asked him while unpacking the first basket.

"No," he admitted, but could anticipate her next question. "I'm fine. My sister and her fiancé are having dinner with Pa and me tonight. We always eat well when she cooks."

"I see." She stacked the dishes in a washbasin. "How is your father? Feeling better, I hope."

"He has his good days and his bad." He felt the need to

explain Pa's lousy behavior. "Unfortunately, he and Dorothy met on a bad day."

"I agree," Junie murmured. Taking out the last dish, she said, "Why don't you go to the parlor, and I'll call down Dorothy."

The urge to escape out of the kitchen's back door gripped him. "There's no need to if she's busy. I don't want to disturb her."

"She'll welcome the break in dusting, I'm sure." Junie went to the hall and stood at the bottom of the stairs. "Dottie Mae, you have a guest." Creaking floorboards let them know Dorothy had heard the summons, and Junie winked at Eldon. "Excuse me, won't you?"

She left before he could reply, but he couldn't care as Dorothy descended. She gave him a thin smile while saying, "Hello, Eldon. Is there something I can help you with? How are the children? Have they left Madison, yet?"

He looked up at her, reminded of why he adored her so much. Even angry and hurt, she was the most beautiful woman in the world. "No, they're all napping, or were when I left."

"Sister Agatha?" she asked, still terse but motioning him to follow her into the parlor.

"Napping, too, believe it or not," he said. Dorothy's surprise matched how he'd felt when seeing the nun's mouth agape. "I suspect the stagecoach made the woman irrational and sour today."

"I suppose." She sat an ornate chair and motioned for him to do the same. "Was that why your father became so irritated with me?"

Eldon found a place to sit. "He was more upset with me than you."

"Maybe, but it was my reputation he maligned, not yours." She folded her hands in her lap. "I've done nothing but guard my good name all of my life. I've worked hard to be a good teacher and a credit to my family. But to what end? I've had a nun and your father both treat me like a common strumpet when I've been well behaved for most of my life."

The slight disclaimer caught his attention. "For most of your life?"

She nodded, not meeting his eyes. "Well, there were a few pranks I played in school. And a kiss on my front porch that I'll never forget or regret."

"Nor will I." He leaned forward, sitting on the edge of the chair. "Was ours your first kiss? Don't be afraid to answer truthfully. It's all right if you've kissed someone before me."

She glanced up at him with a grin before blushing. "You're the first man I've kissed."

He struggled to keep from cheering. Instead, he slipped

from the chair to kneel. "Dorothy, I have to be honest. I want to be the last man you ever kiss, too." He reached out and took her hand. "I want to marry you, and I suspect you want to marry me as well."

She still didn't look directly at him, but at where he held her hand. "Yes, I admit I'm completely besotted by you."

"Good." He squeezed her fingers with his, joy filling his heart. "We'll marry on any day you choose, even if it's tomorrow."

"Does this mean your father has changed his mind about me?" she asked in a slightly clipped tone. "And will he apologize for calling me a strumpet in public?"

Eldon froze, loath to tell her the brutal truth. He couldn't propose in one breath, however, and then say an outright lie. "I, um, Pa, and I haven't talked since. He won't speak to me at all. Not a word."

Dorothy slid her fingers from his grip. "Then I can't marry you. I won't be the cause of a familial rift."

Fighting the rising panic in his check, Eldon tried, "But he's old, bitter, and has nothing to do with how I feel for you."

She stood, moving toward the hall. "I understand, but I won't be the reason you never see him again. Not only that, but I want his blessing on our marriage." She opened the front door. "When he gives his approval, I'll know he doesn't mean the hurtful things he'd said last night after all."

Unable to believe Dorothy was indicating he should leave, Eldon followed her but couldn't make himself leave the house. "I'm not sure Pa will bless anything I want to do. Since Ma's death, he's been angry at the world and everything in it."

"A man's grief is a powerful thing, I know." Dorothy paused for a few seconds before continuing. "Mother mourned my father for years, as did I." She shook her head. "A marriage beginning under such hostility can only grow worse with each frown or sharp retort." She took him by the hand and led him out to the front porch before letting go. "As much as I care for and adore you, Eldon, I won't marry you."

# CHAPTER 13

"Dorothy? Could you get the door?"

Her mother's voice carried through Dorothy's bedroom wall. She'd heard the knock but ignored it, hoping Junie would deal with Eldon herself. "I don't want to," she yelled back.

"I didn't ask your preferences," Junie responded. "Just go."

"All right." She rolled off the bed, taking a look in her dresser mirror. Splotches marred her skin. Her eyes had deep circles underneath. Good. She'd scare Eldon away, and he'd never come back. She straightened her skirt and headed for the door. No more visits from him and hearing him admit his Pa thought she was a loose woman.

The knock sounded again, and before her mother could holler, Dorothy said, "I've got it," and opened the door.

Jerry grinned. "Hello. I've brought the rest of your bedding. Where should I unload it? Here or around back?"

A wagon stood on the road behind him. If Dorothy stood on tiptoes, she could see the stack of blankets over the sideboards. "Here is fine. My mother and Mattie Lou are busy, but I can help."

"No, I can unload everything myself." He went down the stone path. "There's no need for a fine lady like yourself bothering."

She followed him to the wagon. "Nonsense. I'm equipped with two hands."

"So you are." He gave her an armload of bedding before grabbing twice the amount to carry in, too.

Junie came out as they were walking up the path. "Why, you should have said you needed help."

He waited for her to open the front door before following her into the parlor. "I didn't want to bother you, ma'am."

She took the pillows from Jerry with a smile. "I'm never too busy to help a friend."

"Aw, I appreciate that."

Dorothy ducked inside and went to the kitchen with her armful. The two definitely enjoyed each other's company. She'd never imagined her mother finding love, but then, anything was possible. She returned to the wagon to make sure they'd retrieved everything. Walking back to the house, she hesitated before stepping on the porch. Going in through the front might lead to her interrupting a conversation. But coming in through the kitchen meant she could help Mattie Lou instead of spending the rest of the day brooding upstairs.

She went around, happy to see new flowers blooming along the east side of their home. Tiny green sprouts filled the vegetable garden. With so much life surrounding her, she couldn't help but feel cheered. A few weeds popped up among the new vegetables. Happy to have a task, she rushed in to drop the bedding before returning to pull the strays.

"Goodness, that man can talk." Junie walked up to her and began helping her weed. "I thoroughly enjoy someone who can keep up their end of a conversation."

Dorothy knelt, struggling with a particularly big dandelion. "You didn't spend much time with him at all."

"No," Junie agreed with a slight smile. "But we've decided to have a visit after church on Wednesday evening."

"I see," Dorothy quipped.

Her mother blushed, adding, "He's a good man and easy to spend time with is all."

"Um-hm," she said, working hard to not tease her mother.

"We've talked about what's been going on at the depot."

She glanced at her daughter before adding, "He told me Eldon proposed to you."

Dorothy's nose stung, and her eyes filled with tears as if all of her strength and resolve meant nothing. "He did," she confessed, "And I refused. I won't marry into a family that hates me."

Junie stood, wiping the dirt from her hands before holding out her arms. "Not even if Eldon loves you?"

She got up and fell into her mother's arms, sobbing. "No. I couldn't turn his family against him."

"There there, darling. I completely understand." Junie patted Dorothy's back to comfort her. "Maybe one day, Mr. Lukeson will change his mind. Would you like me to have a serious discussion with him?"

"No," she replied with a sniff. "I can fight my own battles."

Her mother gave her another hug before letting go. "You can, but you know you're never alone."

Dorothy leaned against Junie. "I know, and thank you."

THE COOL AIR REFRESHED DOROTHY AS SHE LOCKED UP the schoolhouse door. So many children packed into a room meant hot and stuffy afternoons. Thanks to Larry's antics during recess and David's joining in, her chalkboard and erasers were clean and ready for tomorrow. Plenty of time remained between now and Wednesday night church.

In the two, now three days since she'd refused Eldon's proposal, walking past the train station took all of her courage. She expected him to run out and meet her every time. Except, why would he when she'd already given him an answer? Lost in thought, Dorothy didn't even notice Junie coming out of the station in front of her. "Mother?"

Junie whirled around. "Oh! Dotty!"

"Mother..." she warned.

She clamped a hand over her mouth, saying from between her fingers, "Sorry, I forgot myself. Dorothy, I meant, and is it so late?"

"It must be since I'm finished with school for the day." She couldn't resist teasing, "How is Mr. Thompson, anyway?"

Junie sighed and tucked a stray lock of hair behind her ear. "He's fine. Such a nice man too."

After a glance at the depot's front door, Dorothy was reluctant to run into Eldon, too. She took her mother's arm and began walking home. "Must be for you to forget the time. That's not like you."

She went along, replying, "It isn't, but that speaks to how kind of a person and easy to talk to he is."

"I assume our potluck for church tonight is ready," Dorothy commented, happy with the small talk.

Junie stopped dead in her tracks. "Oh heavens, no, it isn't."

"Uh oh," she said, not needing to state the obvious of Wednesdays being Mattie Lou's day off.

"Goodness, and I forgot the mail." She took her daughter by the shoulders. "Darling, you must go back and get my lady's book."

"Now?" she squeaked and left "See Eldon?" unsaid. She argued, "We can't wait until tomorrow?"

"No. I left it on the counter where anyone could take it." Junie put her hands together and begged. "Please?"

Dorothy shook her head. "I can't. What if I see Eldon? It's too soon."

"Maybe so, but it'll hurt like pulling a thorn out quickly. A sting, but better as you walk away from him." A church bell began to chime the hour, and Junie frowned. "Please. Just grab our magazine and come home. With any luck, he'll be in the back, hiding from you, too."

"Mother," she began.

Junie hurried away with a wave. "Don't dawdle, or you'll be late for church."

Dorothy sighed, vastly irritated at her mother's apparent manipulations. Junie wanted her and Eldon to talk. She was sure of it. Well, retrieving a magazine didn't mean she needed to even see him, just dart in and run out in a few seconds. She lifted her chin and went into the train station. As she entered the cool building, a train's whistle sounded, warning of its approach. If she timed it correctly, she'd be back out before the crowds swarmed inside.

Jerry wasn't at his usual spot, and she didn't see Eldon anywhere. With good luck, she'd be on her way home in a few seconds. Her footsteps echoed in the empty building until she slowed down and focused on treading lighter. Her hand on the magazine, the back doors opened, and Jerry strolled in. A crowd of people followed him. He grinned. "Well, hello, Miss McLean. I see you found your mother's magazine."

Caught and frozen in place, she replied, "I did, thank you," while backing up to leave.

"Eldon, you have a customer," Jerry hollered. "He'll be right out." He reassured her with a sly grin.

"I'll be right out," Eldon replied from the far end of the mailroom.

"See?" Jerry said.

Dorothy couldn't help but chuckle. Clutching her magazine, she shook her head, ignoring the tingles Eldon's voice gave her. "I should probably go now."

"Stay," Jerry said as quiet as the noisy room allowed. "Talk to him one last time, and if your mind doesn't change, you never have to come back."

Before she could reply, Eldon walked out of his mailroom. Surprise and longing flashed across his face before calmness settled in. "Hello, Miss McLean. Whatever you need will have to wait until after I retrieve the mail bags from the platform."

"I don't need anything, Mr. Lukeson," she replied in what she hoped was a neutral tone.

A young and rather attractive man came forward and asked, "Excuse me, did you say McLean and Lukeson?"

Jerry nodded. "We did, can we help you?"

"Actually, you already have." He dug in his jacket pocket and pulled out a card. "My name's Thomas Grant, and I'm with the Blessed Heart Orphanage. I'm thrilled to meet you both." He reached out to shake Eldon's hand. "You two are all the children could talk about once they reached Kansas City. I don't think I've ever heard such clever stories about rabbits, either."

Dorothy laughed, her face burning. "I'm to blame for that and hope you don't mind too much."

"I was delighted to listen. The children told me about bunnies named Julia, Robby, and Chas, so now I'm curious to hear the other four stories." He faced Eldon. "And you, Mr. Lukeson. The children enjoyed the games you invented for them, too. In fact, due to their positive comments, I'm sure when you're both married, we'll accept your applications as adoption agents for our orphanage."

"Oh—" Dorothy began.

Eldon cut in, saying, "We're not planning on getting married, I'm afraid."

His voice saying the words out loud cut through her heart. Her mother was wrong. All of this hurt far worse than any rosebush's thorn could. Nothing she could ever do would heal this deep ache in her chest. In an instant, she realized she couldn't live the rest of her life without being his wife. Dorothy lifted her chin and blurted, "Yes." She stared at Eldon, daring him to defy her. "Yes, we are planning on getting married."

Mr. Grant chuckled and clapped Eldon on the back. "I'm glad to hear it. With Lukeson's work in the station and Miss McLean's teaching abilities, you would make a terrific duo."

Dorothy nodded at Eldon, still daring him to disagree. "I've always thought so. When we first met several years ago in school, I was enamored of him but didn't dare to even smile when he said hello." Her heart pounded so hard, she knew it would jump out of her body. Still, she had to let him know how much she loved him. "Every moment since I first saw Mr. Lukeson, I've fallen even deeper in love with him."

Eldon tilted his head, frowning. "But my family has been a problem in us choosing a date to marry."

She smiled, a little nervous because he was right. "That's why we've wanted a long engagement. I've thought about maybe marrying in December since everyone will be ready for the holidays and in a better mood."

Mr. Grant nodded. "Excellent choice since the nights would be longer, too."

Dorothy wasn't quite naïve because Junie believed forewarned was forearmed. Still, long nights spent as Eldon's wife left her face far too hot in the cool room. She struggled to meet Mr. Grant's eyes and gave a quick glance at Eldon. "Oh, I'd not considered such a thing, but December sounds far better than any day in summer."

"I agree," Mr. Grant replied as the train's whistle rang out. "That's my signal to leave. Before I go, do contact me when or if you're interested in helping place orphans in the area. So many children need good homes."

"Thank you," Eldon replied. "We'll keep your offer in mind."

The agent gave a little salute before walking away. The moment he cleared the doors, Eldon turned to her. "Winter and long nights, hmm? Was that all talk, or did you mean it?"

"Excuse me," Jerry said, leaving his counter. "I need to help with the train."

Once he was out of earshot, Dorothy stepped closer to Eldon. "I meant it. Every word."

He searched her face, putting his hands on her shoulders. "You refused me when I asked, Dorothy. Why, if you'd planned on a December wedding? Or am I delusional and you're marrying someone else?"

Dorothy caressed his face, the late afternoon stubble rough against her palm. "I've only been proposed to by one man, and he's the same one I wished I'd accepted."

He took her in his arms, giving her lips the briefest of kisses. "And if you formally accepted my proposal, would you want to wait seven long months or marry sooner?"

"My heart says I want to marry you tonight, but my mind disagrees," she replied. As Eldon's smile faded, she rushed to say, "I want the extra time to convince your father I'm the perfect woman for you."

He chuckled, his eyes looking at her with love. "Pa isn't the one who'll be living with you, Dorothy. I will. What I want with you matters far more than anything he says."

"I'm glad you think so strongly in my favor." She gave him a kiss. "I also think being cuddled up with you during a blizzard on our wedding night sounds very appealing."

Pulling her closer, he asked, "So you'll agree to be my wife in December, no matter what happens?"

"Yes, Eldon." She stared him in the eyes, meaning each word. "Even if my mother disowns me for missing church tonight. Even if your father kicks you out of your home for marrying a loose woman like me. Even if Jerry ever stops eavesdropping. I'll marry you by the end of the year. I promise."

Eldon picked her up off of the ground and twirled her around. Kissing all over her face, he paused barely long enough to say, "I have a feeling by the time our first baby is born, Pa will think of you as his daughter."

Babies? Dorothy laughed, too shy to even consider what must happen before then. "I hope so, but as long as you love me, I'll be happy."

He took her face in his hands. "My darling, I love you more than any law should allow and will for the rest of our lives. I'm already the happiest man in the world because you love me."

## ABOUT THE AUTHOR

With an overactive imagination and a love for writing, I decided to type out my daydreams and what if's. I currently live in Kansas City with my husband and a few cats. When not at the computer, I'm supposed to be in the park for a jog and not buying everything in the yarn store's clearance section.

Find me online at https://twitter.com/LauraLStapleton, https://www.facebook.com/LLStapleton, and at http://lauralstapleton.com. Subscribe to my newsletter to keep up on the latest and join my Facebook group at Laura's Favorite Readers.

Made in United States
North Haven, CT
13 June 2024